*A
Harlequin
Romance*

OTHER
Harlequin Romances
by SUSAN BARRIE

Many of these titles are available at your local bookseller,
or through the Harlequin Reader Service.

For a free catalogue listing all available Harlequin Romances,
send your name and address to:

HARLEQUIN READER SERVICE,
M.P.O. Box 707, Niagara Falls, N.Y. 14302.
Canadian address: Stratford, Ontario, Canada.

or use order coupon at back of book.

BRIDE
IN WAITING

by

SUSAN BARRIE

HARLEQUIN BOOKS

TORONTO   •   WINNIPEG

First published in 1961 by Mills & Boon Limited,
17 - 19 Foley Street, London, England.

SBN 373-01526-7

Harlequin Canadian edition published September, 1971
Harlequin U.S. edition published December, 1971

Printed in Canada

CHAPTER I

THE flat seemed very empty as April moved about it. In Señora Cortez' bedroom her hastily denuded dressing-table was still thick with powder, and there were one or two dresses hanging up in the wardrobe, but otherwise the room was completely changed. Not even the heavy scent of French perfume could bring Señora Cortez back to the room as a regular occupant.

Of the dresses she had said disdainfully, as she cast them aside:

"I shall not require them. My husband chose them, and I dislike them intensely, so you can have them. They're about your size, and they'll see you through a few parties if you're thinking of going gay during the next few weeks."

Not a word about the many weeks of salary owing to April, or the price of her fare home to England. Presumably she had been leaving these pertinent matters to her husband to be dealt with, but Señor Cortez had flounced out of the flat in the early hours, and the only message he had left behind had been to the effect that he was flying to Brazil. When Señora Cortez saw the message she shrugged her shoulders.

"And *I* am flying to New York!" she said. "So that makes two of us clearing out of this torrid place. Three, because I shall not leave Juan behind!"

Juan was the little boy, with very large eyes and

engaging milk-white baby teeth, for whom April had been engaged as a kind of nanny-companion-governess.

It was certainly very hot in Madrid at that fiercest of all seasons of the year. August, in England, can be mellow with the approach of autumn, but in central and northern Spain it seems to reach boiling point around that month. It could be one reason why tempers had flared so the night before, after the dinner party guests had departed, and the host and hostess who had looked so elegant presiding at opposite ends of the flower-decked table had resorted to throwing things at one another in the huge *sala* that positively reeked of the fragrance of various kinds of exotic tobaccos and expensive feminine perfumes.

As April entered it and saw the overturned coffee tables and flower vases lying on end, magazines scattered like withered leaves and liqueur glasses ground into the carpet, she experienced a sharp sense of distaste. The Señor and Señora had done the job thoroughly. They had quarrelled with a violence that had sounded really alarming to the girl who had already gone to bed, and was trying to get to sleep with the sheet pulled up over her ears. They had stormed at one another in a mixture of English and Spanish—with a few Americanisms thrown in, for Señora Cortez was from Philadelphia—and, when it seemed that the battle was at its height, Señora Cortez had rushed through into her bedroom and started dragging at suitcases and banging at wardrobe doors until the whole flat shook with her frenzy.

Still in her evening gown of black lace over apricot satin, with diamonds in her ears and sparkling at her throat, she had appeared at April's door and informed

6

her that she was leaving . . . leaving just as she was! Her husband had already shaken the flat further with his slamming of the front door, and it didn't matter to her in the least that she might never see him again. She was flying home to her parents in America, and that was what mattered.

She was flying home to her parents in America, and she would sue for divorce at the very earliest possible moment. A stream of vituperation directed against her husband left her lips, and April was horrified. She had known for some time that Venetia and Pedro Cortez were on the verge of breaking up—two such opposite temperaments, Latin and blatantly American, could not possibly get along together for long — but she hadn't dreamed the break-up would be so sudden.

And on top of an apparently successful dinner party too!

But it was the dinner party that had brought about the crisis. Pedro had accused Venetia of flirting with one of the guests, and she hadn't denied it. Furthermore, he had accused her of doing so in front of a particularly important guest, and that was the last straw. Don Carlos de Formera y Santos was an old and close friend of the Cortez family, and in the best Spanish circles there were methods of behaving, and methods by which one was judged and found wanting if one had the bad taste to follow them and flout old and valued traditions by staring them insolently in the face.

Venetia hadn't merely stared them in the face, she had tossed them carelessly over her shoulder. She had found Don Carlos de Formera y Santos an acute bore, and told her husband so. He might be the richest man in the world—the most successful man, with the

7

bluest of blood in his veins—but every time he looked at her down his aristocratic straight nose, and out of his dark disapproving eyes, she had wanted to scream because she was quite sure he was finding a lot wanting in her, and a lot of other things he couldn't approve of besides.

Part of the battle that had raged had been over Don Carlos, and others of his kind who behaved exactly like him... stiff-necked, formal, unimaginative Spaniards, who liked their women to be stiff-necked, formal, and unimaginative too.

Venetia had declared that she was tired of trying to conform to a pattern of life for which she was quite unsuited. She was tired of formality and primness, unvarying correctness, stupidity and dullness. The women of Spain had only two interests... their husbands and their children. They had no conversation outside these two interests, and their minds became atrophied before they were out of their twenties. Venetia was determined that hers should not become atrophied, and she was determined to escape from the heat, the dust, and the monotony of Madrid. The vicious flare-up with her husband provided her with an excuse, and while April looked on with detached amazement—somewhat sleepy amazement too, since she had not yet been permitted to close her eyes—her employer literally tore off her splendid dress, designed by a top couturier in Madrid, scrambled into something suitable for travel, lifted her child bodily out of his cot and dressed him too, and then telephoned for a taxi. And at such an unseasonable hour that was rather a lengthy process.

In between abusing the operator, the night porter, local taxi services, and—above all!—the dreadful

Spanish lethargy which prevented one getting anything done quickly, Venetia Cortez issued a few random instructions to the English girl.

"You can stay here for the next few days, if you like. At least until you've got your own journey home fixed. If you've got any sense you won't take another job in Spain."

April said a little awkwardly:

"But I . . . I'm not at all sure I've got enough money to pay for my fare home!"

This was no more than the truth. The Cortez' owed her quite a bit, for although they lived well and luxuriously, the original arrangement for paying her her salary monthly had been allowed to drift into a policy of supplying her with a cheque at some distant future date. And the little money she had had when she went to them had been exhausted by the need for clothes, and various other small expenses. In her handbag, at that moment, April had about five pounds in English money, and perhaps another five pounds in Spanish *pesetas*.

Venetia made an expressive gesture with her hands. She had learned a lot of Spanish gestures since she became a Spaniard's bride.

"Oh, don't worry. Pedro is bound to return within a few hours; even though he says he's flying off to Brazil. As far as I know he's taken practically nothing with him."

"And supposing he doesn't return?" April voiced the possibility quietly.

Venetia looked at her in some astonishment.

"Return? Of course he will! He has this flat to dispose of, and all that sort of thing. And he's bound to remember that we haven't paid you for ages." Mild curiosity crossed her face. "How many weeks' money are owing to you?"

"About twelve," April told her.

Venetia's feathery eyebrows rose. She was a butterfly personality, eager to be on the move, eager to be doing something fresh always. And her pretty, uninteresting face was restless too. For one instant she looked vaguely uncomfortable.

"It's rather a lot, isn't it?" she admitted. "But don't worry . . . Pedro may bore me to death, but he isn't dishonest. He won't rook you of your wages." She fumbled with the clasp of her handbag. "I'd pay you myself, but I've got to be sure I've enough money to settle all my own expenses . . . and Juan's. You can't take risks with a child."

"But you could wait until it's absolutely certain Señor Cortez intends to return to the flat," April suggested.

Venetia was galvanized into further activity by the suggestion.

"Not on your life! I wouldn't be here when he comes back for a . . . a million dollars! I've finished with him!" She fumbled once more with her handbag. "Here, take this." A tiny roll of lower denomination notes fell at April's feet. "They won't get you far, but they're something. And if you're really in a fix you can always go to the Consul . . . That's what Consuls are for!"

Then, as she heard the taxi drive up outside, she grabbed a her crocodile dressing-case, and a jewel-case made of shagreen, with a heavy gold clasp and gold initials. She took the somnolent Juan by the hand.

"I must go. Thanks for all you've done for Juan, and ... good-bye!"

And, before April could attempt to give a final, farewell hug to the little boy, she had gone, the flat door had closed behind her, and April was standing in the middle of the hall in her dressing-gown, looking and feeling completely bewildered.

When the servants failed to turn up in the morning she wondered whether the news had gone round that Señor and Señora Cortez had fled. She wondered, also, how much money was owing to the domestic staff.

She wandered through the flat, after making herself some coffee for breakfast, and wondered what her next move should be, and what on earth she was going to do if Pedro Cortez failed to return.

But he had always struck her as a solid, dependable type. Perhaps a little too solid, for he was running to flesh, but sincere and rather pathetically devoted to his wife and son. It was going to be a bad blow to him when he discovered they were neither of them likely to be restored to him for some considerable while, unless he held some card he could play to induce Venetia to return. And, even if that happened, the quarrels would re-commence, and the bickerings.

It was not a pleasant atmosphere for a young child to grow up in.

April put away some of Juan's toys, and tidied the nursery. The nursery-maid usually made her appearance about eight o'clock, but, along with the cook and the sleek manservant, she was conspicuous this morning by her absence.

The dining-room was a depressing sight with the long table still loaded with china and glass and high-

11

piled dishes of fruit, to say nothing of wilting flowers. April threw open the windows and then closed the shutters against the fierce assault of the morning sunshine, already strong enough to be an enemy if one was out of doors in it without a hat or a pair of dark glasses.

The streets of Madrid were alive with glare, the pavements hot enough to blister sandalled feet. Yet many pairs of feet hurried over them towards offices and shops, that would be closed during the even fiercer heat of the afternoon. In the fashionable shopping-centre, where streets like the Gran Via, San Jeronimo and the Alcala attracted numbers of fashionable women during the few short hours when shopping was feasible, the doors were already being opened to intrepid purchasers.

But the smell of hot dust, spicy flowers and weary humanity that rose up with the echoing patter of feet caught at April's tired throat, and made her wonder still more—and with a mounting sense of depression—what was ahead of her during the next few hours, and why such an unenviable situation should have arisen and why she should be the one who had to cope with it.

Her first job abroad, and she hadn't even been dismissed from it... It had suddenly ceased to exist!

She pushed the hair back from her brow—heavy dark brown hair that she wore a little longer than was strictly fashionable—and regarded her own reflection in a mirror with worried, soft brown eyes. The combination of brown hair and golden-brown eyes was unusual in Spain, and therefore immediately striking, for Spanish men and women tend to a great depth of darkness when their eyes are dark... which they very nearly always are. And eyes the colour of pale amber —as limpid as pools—are a distinct rarity.

And, allied to luxurious, silky brown eyelashes, a perfect English complexion, as yet unaffected by the heat of Madrid, and features as clear-cut as an old-fashioned cameo, the effect was sufficiently arresting almost always to arouse interest.

Since coming to Madrid she had grown used to being stared at by amorous young men, but she was too free from conceit to realize fully why they stared. Just as she was too instinctively honest and uncomplicated to be capable of leaving anyone in the kind of temporary fix in which she appeared to have been left.

For, if the worst came to the worst, she could, of course, go to the Consul ... But what an extraordinary position to have to explain!

The Cortez furniture was heavy and massive, the furnishings far too sumptuous, and by the time the morning had worn itself out she was beginning to feel slightly revolted by the very sight of it. She put away Señora Cortez' dresses—determined never to wear them herself—packed her own clothes in readiness for immediate departure just as soon as Señor Cortez returned, consumed a light lunch in the kitchen, drowsed through the appalling heat of the afternoon, and then heard the telephone ring about six o'clock.

She fairly raced to it, her heart beating suffocatingly with relief.

"Yes?" she said into the mouthpiece.

A cool, clipped, masculine voice answered in Spanish.

"Who is that?"

"April Day," she answered—conscious of the absurdity of the name as she did so. "I am employed by Señora Cortez to look after her little boy. Or rather,' she amended confusedly, sick with disappointment because it was not Señora Cortez, "I was ... I'm not now!"

"And why not?" the calm voice weighted with logic demanded.

"Because Señora Cortez is no longer here ... and neither is her little boy."

"You mean they've gone away suddenly on some sort of a holiday?"

"Oh no, they've gone . . . for good!"

"Indeed?" But the voice was quite unruffled. "And Señor Cortez?"

"I—I'm waiting for him to come back." Her voice caught with nervousness, and waves of agitation went out over the wire. "He—he left first, you see ... I mean, there was a quarrel ..."

"And at this precise moment you are alone in the flat?"

"Yes. I don't know what's happened to the servants, but I am alone."

"So!" the deliberate voice said levelly, as if he was pondering the matter. "I rang to confirm a luncheon arrangement for tomorrow that I made with Señor Cortez last night, but if he is not there it doesn't matter. That is to say, it is of no particular consequence. But the fact that you are alone is of some consequence. I will be with you in a little less than a quarter of an hour."

It was, actually, not any longer than ten minutes when he drove up to the entrance of the block of flats. April, watching from a window—although carefully screened by a curtain—saw him alight from a magnificent long cream car, which he had driven himself, and ascend the short flight of steps to the front door. She recognized him at once as Don Carlos de Formera y Santos, and within a matter of seconds he was whisked up in the lift, and a bare few seconds after that his long, firm index finger was pressing the bell of the flat door.

CHAPTER II

APRIL had to steel herself before opening the door. She suddenly felt acutely nervous at the thought of coming face to face with someone like Don Carlos, whom she had never actually spoken to—except under somewhat extraordinary circumstances ten minutes before over the telephone—and admitting him to an empty flat. By conventional Spanish standards that was, for one thing, an unconventicnal thing to do, and Don Carlos was extremely conventional.

"Good evening, *señorita*," he said, as he stepped purposefully past her ito the hall.

He was wearing an impeccable light grey suit, and to her astonishment she saw that he was also wearing an Old Etonian tie. So he was a Spaniard who had been educated at Eton! And although he had not, so far, spoken anything but Spanish to her, she felt certain his English was perfect.

He proved it by looking down at her with controlled curiosity from his infinitely superior height and stating more or less bluntly:

"You are Miss Day. You said that your name was April Day. It is unusual."

She felt herself colouring ridiculously.

"It isn't a name I would have chosen for myself," she confessed. "I mean," at his look of surprise, "the combination of April and Day is too obvious, isn't it?"

"Is it?" he said. "But the obvious is not necessarily

16

something to be avoided. And my memories of an April day in England are very pleasant."

He looked about him at the empty hall, noting the slight film of dust on the highly polished furniture, and the flowers that had not been replaced, although April had seen to it that they had fresh water.

"So you are quite alone here," he remarked.

"Yes," April replied.

He walked towards the door which led into the main *sala,* and she followed him, apologizing for the confusion, although here again she had made an endeavour to restore order.

"This is all quite extraordinary," Don Carlos observed, drawing forward for her one of the satin-seated chairs. "Your employers were here with you last night, yet this morning they both departed without, apparently, giving you any clear idea when you can expect their return?"

His hard dark eyes were on her, the line of his lips compressed.

"Is that so, *señorita*?"

April admitted that it was so. She found she was clenching her hands rather tightly together in her lap.

"You said something about a quarrel when you spoke to me on the telephone. Without revealing any secrets of your employers—if you are in possession of them, which I should doubt!—will you give me some idea what that quarrel was about?"

April hesitated. Señora Cortez had kept few secrets from her, and the quarrel had been so vulgar and blatant that everyone in the flat must have known what it was about before it was ended. And perhaps

17

that accounted for the extraordinary disinclination to return to duty of the domestic staff.

"It was a rather serious boiling up of the usual quarrel," she said awkwardly, looking anywhere but at the somewhat accusing directness of his eyes. And what eyes they were, handsome, black, and as unrevealing as the darkest hour of an exceptionally dark night. "Señor and Señora Cortez are not often in agreement . . . or that is an impression I formed of them after being with them only a few weeks! They —as we would say in England—seem to grate on one another, and last night the edginess got the better of them." She knew she was giving voice to the understatement of the year, but he did not look the type of man who would consider deliberate emphasis a good thing . . . particularly when it concerned a couple of his friends. "Señora Cortez rather flew off the handle when the Señor said something that annoyed her."

"Indeed?" He sounded as if he was just a little surprised. "And have you any idea what it was that the Señor said that caused the Señora to take so much exception to it that she packed her bags and left without giving any reasonable warning to anyone?"

"Yes." She eyed him steadily . . . or tried to do so. "But it's their affair, and I don't wish to repeat anything I heard last night. Naturally, I was not expected to overhear, and I'd prefer to keep silent, if you don't mind, *señor*."

He nodded dryly.

"As you please. A good employee respects his, or her, employers' confidence, but this would not appear to be a case in which any particular confidence was reposed in you. You, unfortunately, overheard rather more than you wanted to overhear, or so I gather, and in addition you appear to have been left holding the baby . . . as I feel sure you would also say in England!"

She coloured, but admitted ruefully:

"Unfortunately, there isn't any baby left for me to hold. My charge has been taken away from me!"

"Little Juan, you mean? The whole thing is quite incredible, and unless you are making a grave mistake, so reprehensible that I feel bereft of words! For a child to be snatched from his cot in the middle of the night and taken by his mother on an air flight to America, while his father proceeds by a different route to a somewhat more southerly destination, without any intention whatsoever of being reunited with his family, is beyond my comprehension at this moment! Are you sure, *señorita*," sternly, "that you are not making a mistake? I was to have lunch with Señor Cortez tomorrow, and although I have always thought Señora Cortez a little unsuited to him—she is too young, and too much imbued with the American idea of marriage to have gained my entire approval—I would, nevertheless, not easily believe it of her that she could break up a home so suddenly."

"But it was Señor Cortez who left the flat first," April said quickly, defensively, amazed at the slight but definite feeling of resentment which stirred in her because he referred to a woman who spoke her own language in such under-valuing terms. And Venetia Cortez was at least a couple of years older than herself. "He said that he was flying off to Brazil, and he didn't even bother to take any of his things with him. He just slammed out of the flat!"

"Then it's highly likely he'll be back," Don Carlos said briskly.

April looked doubtful.

"Then why hasn't he telephoned? It's hours since he and the Señora had their quarrel, and she told him plainly enough that she was leaving... for good! She also made it perfectly clear that she was taking Juan with her. If he has any real concern for either of them —and, despite the awful upset, I'm sure he has!— you'd think he'd want to find out whether she carried out her threat, and at least get someone to telephone. That is, if he was merely bluffing about not coming back, and is still in Madrid."

Don Carlos frowned.

"But you don't think he is?"

"I think he was too angry to bluff. I think he went and got himself the first avaitable seat on an aircraft leaving for Brazil, and will probably do business there, and come back when his temper has cooled sufficiently to allow him to do so."

Don Carlos frowned still more.

"Has he interests in Brazil? I know little about him. We met quite by accident."

"Oh, yes—quite big business interests."

"And you think it would have been quite a simple matter for him to pick up his passport at his office, perhaps a few essential documents as well, and disappear into the blue?"

"Temporarily, yes," April answered.

"And, in the meantime, what is to happen to you?" he asked shrewdly, those black eyes concentrating full upon her. "Did Señora Cortez give you to understand that she no longer required your services?"

"Yes, but she expected me to wait here until the Señor returned. She was of the opinion that he would do so."

"Why? When he had so clearly expressed his own intention of doing nothing of the kind!"

"There were certain things to be attended to. Certain ... matters."

"Such as?"

"My—my salary, for one thing. The Señora herself could not attend to it."

"And a certain sum over and above your salary, I would say, as recompense for losing your employment so suddenly, and through no fault of your own." He was frowning suddenly, and quite noticeably. " Do you really mean to tell me that the Señora actually left his flat without dealing with such an important thing as your salary, how, and by what means, you were to return home to England, and so forth, although she had no absolute certainty that her husband would return? That she left you here to wait ... indefinitely?"

April felt her flush beginning to burn her cheeks, and she realized that she was blushing a little for Venetia Cortez.

"She was very upset," she ventured. "I don't think she quite realized what she was doing."

He uttered a sound that was obviously the Spanish equivalent of "What utter rubbish!"

"And you, who are in a strange country, are supposed to know what you are doing? Although you are without the money you have earned, and are put to the necessity of finding fresh employment! The whole story grows even more incredible as you unfold it to me! I have already confessed that my opinion of Señora Cortez was never high ... but this is something I would not have believed of her!"

He stood up and started to pace about the room,

21

and his frown was so black that it faintly alarmed April.

"I am going to put to you a few questions," he said, "and you must answer them truthfully, and without embarrassment. How much money does this absconding family owe you? How much *altogether* is owing to you?"

She told him, and he pursed his lips.

"How about your fare to England? Would that have been included in the final settlement?"

"I—I imagine so. It was part of the arrangement when I came out here nine months ago."

"And how much money have you yourself? With you in this country, that is. Enough to get you home to England?"

She shook her head.

He stood quite still in front of her, looking down at her and the thick waves of shining hair that caught and imprisoned the brilliant evening sunshine . . . or as much of it as found its way through the still partially closed shutters.

"Then what, may I ask, were you intending to do . . . if I hadn't telephoned?"

She shook her head again, rather helplessly.

"There . . . there is always the Consul, isn't there? The British Consul."

"There is," he agreed, and started his fierce pacing about the room again.

When he came back to her the second time it was quite obvious he had made up his mind about something.

"One thing you cannot do, *señorita*," he said, speaking briskly, "is remain here in this flat. Whether or not Señor Cortez is likely to return doesn't enter into it. Although—and I am astounded that this did not occur to Señora Cortez!—if he did return while the servants are still absent it would be most improper that you should be here. I have no doubt at all that he will deal with the question of your salary in time, but in the meantime you must allow me to think and act for you. I will see that you are installed in an hotel without further delay."

April started to protest, but he cut short her few brief utterances.

"There is no alternative, Miss Day. I regret that you have been placed in this impossible position, but it can be remedied, and will be—at once! Can you collect together a few of your things, and we will leave as soon as you are ready. The rest of your possessions I will arrange to have collected and delivered to you within as short a time as possible."

April stood up. She still felt she must protest, but Don Carlos de Formera y Santos declined absolutely to listen. He held up a shapely, slim brown hand as a silencer.

"Hurry, please, *señorita!* The situation is unconventional enough as it is, and we must not prolong it. I will wait for you here in the *sala,* and the moment you are ready we will leave. It is fortunate that, at this hour of the day, we may do so without notice, for the time of siesta is over and most people are abroad enjoying the cooler air. With any luck, too, the lift attendant may be temporarily off duty."

April gazed at him in mild astonishment. Why was it so essential that they should leave the flat unnoticed?

And then the answer occurred to her at once. This was Madrid, the capital of highly conventional Spain,

23

and Don Carlos was an exceptionally conventional Spaniard. A man of proud family and ancient lineage, who never put a foot wrong if he could possibly avoid it, he liked to see to it that others never put a foot wrong either. At least, when they were temporarily in his charge.

And at the thought another followed it like lightning, and she wondered whether she ought to refuse to involve him in her affairs. For, should they run into any of his friends, it might strike them as odd that he was escorting her, and cause embarrassment. To him, but not to her, for she was wholeheartedly grateful that he had appeared when he did, and that was one reason why she couldn't summon up the strength of mind to refuse his offer of seeing her to an hotel, and placing her once more in security.

She could only hurry away to her room, and start to cram a few things hastily into a suitcase.

CHAPTER III

BUT unfortunately for Don Carlos the lift-man was not only on duty, but he hastened to relieve him of April's suitcase, and insisted on carrying it out to his car and placing it very carefully in the boot. He was intensely obsequious, and looked at April a little inquiringly.

She had seen him almost daily for nearly nine months, and she felt she had to say a polite good-bye to him, a friendly good-bye.

"The señorita is not returning?" he said, in some surprise, and she shook her head.

"I'm afraid not, Miguel. *Adios*," she added.

In the car Don Carlos sat with a slightly inscrutable face behind the wheel. He handled the huge cream roadster beautifully, but he looked at that moment as if he was hardly enjoying his task.

"That was unfortunate," he remarked. "It was unfortunate, also, that you had to enter into conversation with Miguel. Better that he should have been left in the dark as to your movements."

"But he naturally wondered——" she began, and was once more silenced by his upraised hand.

"That is so! But to a menial one does not always offer explanations." Was there cold reproof in his voice, she wondered, or was it just cold? "However, the harm is done now, and there is small point in worrying about it. Miguel is of no importance."

April sat feeling curiously disturbed in the sumptuous seat beside him, and she was glad when they drew up outside one of Madrid's best known hotels. And then a quick qualm of anxiety beset her as she wondered how she was ever going to be able to pay the bill. Even a night in this edifice of quiet but opulent luxury would make a serious dint in her limited resources.

But Don Carlos had her by the elbow and was guiding her up the steps.

"I could have chosen somewhere quieter for you, but I am known here," he told her. "In any case, I do not think it greatly matters."

She glanced at him. Before he had been anxious to escape observation, but now he didn't think it mattered.

She said quickly, agitatedly:

"But this is not the sort of hotel I can afford, *señor!* And if I have to remain here for a few days ..."

"If you have to remain here a few days I'm sure you will be comfortable," he returned suavely, and gripped her arm very firmly. "This way, Miss Day. The reception desk is over here."

It was the manager himself who bowed her to the lift after a room had been procured for April. Don Carlos bowed over her hand as ceremoniously as if she was a highly important acquaintance of his, and told her that he would contact her again the following morning. In the meantime she was to make fullest use of the hotel's amenities, and not trouble her head about the Cortez problems. They would, undoubtedly, be sorted out in time, and so would the all-important matter of her salary. He gave her his word about that.

26

"You are very kind, *señor*," she stammered. "I don't know what I would have done if—if you hadn't telephoned..."

He bowed again.

"You had the Consul in mind," he reminded her dryly.

That night she dined alone in her big, airy room, not feeling quite up to confronting a lot of smart Madrileños in the restaurant. And, in her hurry, she had packed nothing suitable for a first appearance in the great dining-room of the hotel.

She felt splendidly alone and gorgeously isolated as she prowled restlessly about her room and its adjoining bathroom, with every sort of modern fitment. There was that air of grandeur that the Spanish love, however, and the modernity was overlaid by rich satin and damask and beautiful inlaid woods. When night closed down, and the stars shone forth, she was able to sit beside one of her festooned windows and watch the night life of Madrid perambulating over the still warm pavements below her.

Young couples went by—engaged couples, who had the right to hold hands—but mostly the girls were in pairs, and the men were in pairs also, or little groups. Courtship is a serious business in Madrid, and casual acquaintance is frowned upon. April knew this, and she knew that the dark-eyed, warm-skinned *señoritas* loved tap-tapping in their high heels through the hot, silky dusk, before the moon rose. And after the moon rose their pale frocks, and the occasional black mantilla, created an illusion of a black and white world... a world in which there were no semitones whatsoever.

The stars burned with a brilliance that was fierce,

suspended like lamps in the sable sky. Trees were dark and mysterious shapes bending slightly in the occasional light breeze, and in the quiet squares of Madrid light streamed from the windows and picked up the shimmer of cars travelling without a sound over the broad roads. Cars that were either black or white, although in the daytime they were multicoloured and gay.

April found herself thinking about Don Carlos de Formera y Santos. He represented a type of Spaniard she had met few of, for her employers had interposed a rigid line between the domestic side of their establishment and the social side. April, since she received a salary—or should have done!—was relegated to the background when guests were received at the flat. The nearest she had ever come to Don Carlos before that afternoon was when she accidentally encountered him in the hall when she was seeing Juan to bed after he had said good night to his parents.

Poor little Juan, she thought, with an ache of sympathy for him. She had grown very fond of him during the nine months he was in her charge, and she would miss him now. She had no real idea what she would do with herself now that she was once more without a job, but some new kind of work was essential. She couldn't afford to exist for longer than a few weeks without earning her living.

Then her thoughts swept back to Don Carlos. Not merely was he a type new to her, but he was a very managing type . . . a dominating type. She had felt quite unable to resist him when he told her to pack her things and accompany him to an hotel, but at the same time she had wanted to resist him. She was quite sure no one ever dared to defy him, but for one wild

moment she had yearned to do so ... if only because
his eyes were so cool and detached—so immeasurably
aloof, as if she herself was barely human, and he was
conscious of feeling irked because he was forced to
devote some of his time to her. And such was his
mental make-up, such his upbringing, such were his
views on women, conventions, and so forth, that he
could no more have turned his back on the problems
of her situation than he could have walked out on a
wife as Señor Cortez had done.

The wife of Don Carlos de Formera y Santos, when
he acquired one—and, so far as April knew, he was a
bachelor, and a much sought-after one at that—could
count upon it that she would never be left (not even
after a burst of temper!) and she would certainly never be permitted to leave her husband. Don Carlos
would not marry her unless she was the type to conform to every intricate detail of the pattern he set for
her, the way of life she must follow. Once married to
him she would be his for life, and there simply
wouldn't be any question about it.

April felt faintly appalled even by the thought of
the woman who would one day be the Don's wife.
Such a lifetime of servitude—and surely that was
what it would be?—affected her like a chill. A cold
breath that blew upon all her own natural instincts.

But to the Don she owed it that she was no longer
sitting waiting in an empty flat for a telephone to
ring, or a key to grate in the lock of the front door. To
the Don she owed it that she was temporarily housed
in a great deal of luxury.

But to the Don she also owed the feeling that she
was nothing more than a nuisance, an unexpected
demand on his well-trained better instincts. Not even

29

an attractive young woman he would condescend to know if he had met her under another set of circumstances that made no appeal to his chivalry.

The next morning he telephoned about eleven o'clock and said that he would be lunching at her hotel, and that he expected her to have lunch with him. At one o'clock—an early hour for lunch in Madrid, and she realized that this was a special concession to her English habits—he arrived, and she went down into the vestibule to meet him.

She had taken a great deal of pains over her appearance, and she could hardly have looked more charming. Her frock was crisp and white and her hair swung softly on her shoulders. She looked, with her fair skin, as if she ought to smell sweetly of lavender water, and, as a matter of fact, she did.

Her hand, when she offered it to him, was slim and cool, with delicate, pearly nails. There was nothing of the ultra-modern young Englishwoman about her, and certainly none of the American slickness that Venetia Cortez had tried to impress her with.

"Buenos dias, señorita," Don Carlos said smoothly. He eyed her for a moment critically. "You slept well?"

"Very well, *señor*," she answered at once. She added with a slight smile, "I could hardly have done anything else. The bed was so superbly comfortable."

He made no reply, but once more took her arm —and she had no doubt this was his habit when escorting women—and led her towards a kind of cool *patio* effect in the very centre of the hotel. Here, in an atmosphere of potted plants and trailing vines, they sipped a pre-lunch apéritif apiece. The Don was immaculately dressed, as on the day before, and he hitched his trousers carefully to avoid marring the crease as he sat down, and she was quite fascinated by the pristine whiteness of his linen, and the lean brown strength of his wrists as they emerged from his shirt cuffs.

"Tell me about yourself, Miss Day," he requested. "You have parents in England?"

She shook her head.

"No. My father died last year, and I hardly remember my mother."

"Is that so?" he murmured, his eyes on her reflectively ... and not once had she seen a glimmer of admiration in them when they rested on her. "And your father followed some sort of a profession?"

"He was a clergyman," she replied, realizing he was trying to get at her status.

"So!" He lighted one of his long, thin Spanish cigarettes, and studied the tip of it when it was alight. "In what part of England did you live?"

"We lived in Devon," she told him. An expression of wistfulness crossed her face. "It seems a long time ago now. So much has happened in a short time ... only a few months! Now I no longer have a home, and my father is dead. It's quite possible I shall never go back to the West Country."

His eyes lifted swiftly to her face.

"And that troubles you? The thought that you may never go back to where you feel you belong? But the world is wide, and you have much to see. You are too young to vegetate ... to rusticate in an English country parish. Your father's death opened a door for you, in the sense that you have already seen Spain. And might I inquire whether or not you have found yourself drawn to this country?"

She thought of the heat and the dust over the past few weeks, the burning cauldron that was Madrid. And then she thought of the starry nights, the heady scent of the flowers, the charm and politeness of ordinary Spanish people. She thought of the beautiful manners of the upper classes—men such as this man she was talking to now!—their dignity, their preoccupation with the sober side of life. Or so it had struck her. Even in the midst of their pleasures they found time to dwell upon death. They flirted with death in the bull-ring, and they looked on it as a spectacle. In the dark depths of most of their eyes there were slumbering fires, and these meant they were quick to change their mood. Their other preoccupation was love... One felt that they would make wonderful lovers.

Although not, perhaps, Don Carlos. April could not imagine him thawing out at all. And as for the rest of Spain—the plains and the mountains and the brilliant coasts, the towns and the villages, the *ferias* and the Holy Weeks and the *corridas*, far beyond the stony suburbs of Madrid—she knew nothing at all about it. Her brief experience had been of Madrid only.

But even so she found herself slowly agreeing that she was drawn to Spain.

"I'm sorry I've got to go home before I've had a chance to see more of it."

"Yes," Don Carlos conceded, "that is a pity."

A woman passed them on her way to the restaurant, and behind her was another younger woman. Both paused for an instant and bowed as Don Carlos stood up with great agility and bowed ceremoniously in return. The older woman curved her lips a little coolly in the merest semblance of a smile, the younger was too shy to raise her eyes.

Don Carlos stood for rather a long moment beside his chair after they had passed, and although April followed the progress of the two members of her sex who were so expensively and exquisitely dressed that she felt a quick pang of envy until they had left the *patio* behind them, she was aware of the way he frowned when he at last resumed his seat.

He said as if he was speaking with sudden difficulty:

"Shall we go into lunch now? It is a little public here, and we shall have more privacy in the restaurant. I have ordered a table to be reserved for me in a corner. Besides, I have something to say to you that will be better said if unlikely to be interrupted."

Mystified, and a little uneasy—even a little apprehensive—April followed him into the restaurant. Their table was partially concealed by an enormous column that soared upwards to the ceiling, and in addition at the base of the column, there was a cascade of flowers and greenery which screened them from curious eyes. Don Carlos ordered quickly and briefly after consulting the menu, and asking April's permission to order for her, and she gathered from his expression once the waiter had departed that, whatever it was he had to say, he was determined to get it over with as quickly as possible.

"Miss Day," he began, after she had taken a nervous sip of the wine that had been poured into her glass, "you do realize that yours is a somewhat unusual position?"

33

She stared at him.

"You mean...? You mean that you haven't yet heard anything of Señor Cortez?"

"Forget Señor Cortez," he answered in a clipped voice. "So far as I know he is now in Brazil, and in any case, the flat is still empty. I paid a special visit to it this morning. But the repercussions of Señor and Señora Cortez' most unusual behaviour are likely to be grim for you. A little—awkward—to say the least!"

She continued to stare, and then she flushed.

"You mean that I am not likely to get my . . . the money that is owing to me?"

He waved an impatient hand, and she had the feeling that he was actually consumed with impatience.

"My dear Miss Day, I said forget Señor Cortez, and I also meant forget the money he owes you. Money is a small point beside the position you are now in. Yesterday afternoon I realized that the consequences of what had happened could be grave. And after a night devoted to pondering your problem I realize that there is only one answer. You were seen leaving the Cortez flat in my company, and the porter was well aware that the flat was empty. There was no one inside it who could possibly chaperone you. You arrive here with a suitcase—again in my company!— and at least two of my closest friends have observed us, to say nothing of the manager and a fair number of casual acquaintances."

April began to look completely bewildered, and then, all at once, she thought she saw what he was driving at. Her face turned scarlet.

"But, Don Carlos," she protested, "aren't you making a mountain out of a very small molehill? I mean..."

"Whether you and I mean the same thing it doesn't alter the outcome," he answered, with grim precision. "In this country there are accepted codes of behaviour, and even in England a young woman still values her reputation, or so I believe." He sounded a little dry, however, as if he was not actually convinced of anything of the sort. "You are a simple young woman who came to this country to take up employment, and having been abandoned you turned to me." He held up that aristocratic hand of his to silence her as she would have burst forth into indignant protests. "There was nothing else you could do, short of becoming involved with the Consulate, and so you turned to me! I was only too happy to be of assistance, but too late I have recognized the dangers in which I have placed you. If you are to retain your good name, and I am to look my friends in the face, you must accept much more than assistance of me. You must accept me as a husband!"

"What!" she gasped.

"I must propose to you formally, and you must accept me. You have no alternative. Will you do me the honour of becoming my wife, Miss Day? Will you allow me to announce our betrothal?"

"You must be mad!" she gasped this time.

For the first time she saw a look of humour invade his eyes. It was, even, much more than humour. It was brief enjoyment of a situation.

"This is the very first time in my life that I have asked a young woman to marry me," he said. "There have been occasions when I have been somewhat close to it, but never before have the words I have just

35

uttered to you been listened to by any member of your sex. I never imagined that, when the time came when I decided I must take a wife, my proposal would evoke the response that I must be mad!"

"But you are," she reiterated, the brilliant colour not merely dying her cheeks but staining her neck as well. She clutched agitatedly at the stem of her wine "There is absolutely no reason why you should do anything so fantastic as ask me to marry you! You've done nothing at all to compromise me, and if your friends believe you have they must be . . ."

She was going to say "mad" again, but he forestalled her.

"They are my friends," he said quietly. "We will leave it at that."

"But you can't possibly *want* to marry me! You know nothing about me!"

"It would seem," he observed, as he cracked a walnut from a dish in front of him between a long finger and thumb, "that I have a lifetime ahead of me to remedy that. I have no doubt there are many interesting discoveries I have to make, and that goes for you too, my dear Miss Day, so please don't say you know nothing about me! The future will take care of our lack of knowledge of one another. Will you marry me? I fear you have no alternative."

She felt a sudden nervous desire to giggle. It was so absurd, he addressed her as "My dear Miss Day," and yet he was suggesting that they get married. Married! How utterly fantastic!

"If you please, *señor,*" she said, repressing the hysterical uprush of amusement with difficulty, "I'm finding it difficult to take you seriously, and yet if you're serious, I—I realize that I ought to be over-whelmed..."

"Why?" he demanded coolly.

She made a gesture with her hands.

"You wouldn't, normally, ask anyone like—like me—to marry you..."

His eyebrows ascended.

"Indeed? And is that so? And yet why should I not ask someone like you to marry me? You are very pleasing to look at—infinitely pleasing, I'm sure most men would agree," with no sign of pleasure in his expression as he uttered the words, however, "and from the little you have told me of yourself your background is not entirely alien to mine. You are a gentlewoman." The word sounded so odd and formal that for the first time it really penetrated to her under-standing that he would not have touched her with a ten-foot pole—as a maid in a house where she had once worked had been in the habit of picturesquely observing—if she had not been what he described as a "gentlewoman."

Not even to save her reputation!

"How old are you?" he asked suddenly, abruptly.

"Twenty-four," she answered.

He sighed with relief.

"In that case there is no necessity for me to ap-proach your nearest relative with a request for your hand before announcing our engagement. And the sooner, I think, that we do announce our engage-ment——"

"But I haven't said——"

He rose with one graceful movement and proceeded to gather up her gloves and handbag for her. He handed them to her, and waited for her to rise.

"No, you haven't," he agreed, "but you can do so tonight, when I take you out to dine. I will call for you about nine o'clock."

The hysteria rushed up in her throat again.

"Thank you, *señor*," she stammered. "T-thank you!"

"You had better make it Carlos," he said casually. For the second time the flash of humour leapt into his eyes. "Even in Spain we make use of Christian names when we contemplate becoming betrothed."

But for the life of her she couldn't imagine him calling her April.

CHAPTER IV

MADRID is by far the highest capital in Europe, and perhaps because it stands so high, and even in the hottest weather there is the sparkle of the mountains underlying its suffocating heat, the night life of Madrid is feverish and active. It begins with the sipping of cocktails at an hour when other capitals are sitting down to dinner, and goes on in gilded clubs and private houses until the dawn, which comes creeping over the Guadarrama in a blaze of splendour.

Then, and then only, do the Madrileños go home to sleep.

April knew little or nothing of the night life of this exotic capital where she had lived for nine months, but she had assisted many times in the toilet of Señora Cortez when she was going out for the evening, and she was well aware of the standard of elegance a woman who was being escorted out to dinner was expected to attain. But whereas Señora Cortez had only to run her hand along a whole line of dresses and make her choice, April had to make up her mind between an extremely simple black silk and a pale rose-coloured crêpe, and neither of them seemed suitable for dining with Don Carlos.

The rose-coloured crêpe was quite lovely, but it was obviously an inexpensive dress, and in it she felt a little foolish when she thought of the evening ahead of her. Rather like the fairy on the Christmas tree, and the women Don Carlos was used to most decidedly had nothing to do with Christmas trees. They were *soignée* and patrician and beautiful—so many young Spanish girls were almost startlingly beautiful—and, nine times out of ten, they wore black.

April decided that her only safe bet was to wear the black, and she was looking a little sombre and subdued in it when her room telephone rang to inform her that Don Carlos was awaiting her below. She picked up a lovely black lace mantilla she had bought in a moment of recklessness and draped it round her shoulders, and went down for the second time that day to meet him. She had given little thought to the proposal he had made her at lunch time—having not the smallest intention of marrying him, however badly he imagined he had compromised her (or she had compromised him, she was not quite sure which)—and was for one moment so much affected by his appearance that it temporarily deprived her of the little sang-froid she had left.

If a man could look beautiful, Don Carlos de Formera y Santos was beautiful in evening dress. He wore a white shell jacket and a black cummerbund, and there was a flesh pink gardenia in his buttonhole. For the first time April really noticed the length of his eyelashes, so thick and black that a woman could have envied them—in fact, they were the only slightly womanish thing about him, for otherwise he was an intensely masculine male—and the clean-cut lines of his shapely mouth. His chin and jaw were strong, but not aggressively so, and he had none of the pallor of so many of his countrymen. His skin was brown and healthy, as if he spent a lot of his time in the open, and courted the sun in other countries apart from his own, and his thick black hair had a fascinating slight wave in it. It was also hair that shone like patent leather.

The strength of the man was in his eyes, in spite of the fact that they were entirely unrevealing eyes, and so was the coldness and the hardness. She judged him to be somewhere in his middle thirties, and as a matrimonial catch he must rate high in Madrid... would rate high wherever he went, for he carried about with him, like a garment, an aura of wealth, assurance, ease and security.

Security with a capital S!... And he had asked April to marry him! For the first time she felt shaken by the thought.

"I wish I had thought to send you flowers, *señorita*," he said, as he took in the severe black and whiteness of her appearance. For her only colour was in her lips, and her swinging dark hair. He frowned. "A pity I was so remiss. But next time I promise you I will not forget."

April followed him out to his car, and uneasily she determined to put an end to this attendance he was dancing on her. It was quite incorrect, as she knew, and there was not the smallest reason why he should waste so much of his time on her. The fact that he had made her a serious proposal only a few hours before still eluded her, and, in any case, one did not accept proposals from men who were utter strangers.

Don Carlos, however exalted his position, would have to be made to understand that.

But the strangest evening of her life began with a dinner in a sumptuous Spanish restaurant that overawed and intrigued her to such an extent that she could think of little to say, and the Don was too occupied attemping to induce her to try various unknown dishes, and awaiting her reactions, that the subject of marriage never once cropped up. Afterwards, when she was feeling oddly exhilarated—and quite unusually relaxed—by the wine and the delicious food, he looked at her and suggested that she might like to go on somewhere where they could watch a cabaret, and thinking·that this was the moment to assure him that he was not under the slightest obligation to entertain her, or spend more money on her, she opened her lips to say as much, but was prevented by him saying swiftly, and just a little commandingly:

"Not yet! We have much to discuss, but for the present I would prefer you to relax and enjoy your evening. I had it in mind to let you see something of our dancing, and hear our flamenco songs. I don't suppose you've had an opportunity to do so before, have you?"

She admitted that she hadn't, and they went on to a fashionable night spot where the décor was so magnificent that it took her breath away, and in an atmosphere heavy with cigarette smoke and exotic perfume she watched for the first time the excitable movements of Andalusian dancers, and was fascinated by the waving castanets, the billowing dresses, the wildness of the famous flamenco music. With someone like Don Carlos sharing the little table on the edge of a glittering floor with her—someone so controlled that not a flicker of his eyelashes betrayed what he was really thinking or feeling—it was impossible to believe that Spaniards were the volatile, emotional people the dances seemed to indicate. On the contrary, if Don Carlos was anything to go by, they were remarkably unemotional.

He ordered a bottle of extremely expensive champagne which April barely sipped at, and explained to her in an undertone the various movements of the dancers, and gave her a brief résumé of the history of flamenco dancing. It seemed to appeal to him in an entirely detached manner, as something to be watched coolly and with much criticism, and without any noticeable enjoyment whatsoever... although around them there was much handclapping in the intervals, and other pairs of dark eyes glowed with excitement and pleasure. And when the lights went up he acknowledged the presence of various acquaintances with stiff little bends of his sleek dark head.

April had the feeling that, in spite of the packed condition of the room, she was the cynosure of many pairs of eyes as she sat there with him on the fringe of the floor. Although they had arrived late they had been bowed at once to this enviable position where they could see without anything getting in the way of their line of vision, and the whole room could observe them if it wished.

She felt as if her black dress was under a kind of microscope, her English colouring the subject of much quiet discussion. She could almost hear these ladies of Madrid discussing her, while diamonds flashed in their ears and on their strikingly white throats and bosoms, and their menfolk tried to provide information as to whom she could possibly be. In England the men would have remained discreetly silent, but Spanish men are almost always intrigued by pale colouring such as April's, and quite a number of the looks directed at her were looks of admiration. These were the masculine ones, and to their wives they endeavoured to explain their obvious interest.

"It is the English *señorita* who has charge of the Cortez son and heir. Pedro Cortez, whose wife is also English..."

"No, American," another man corrected him, and his eyes brightened perceptibly. "A very charming woman... and beautiful!"

"They are all beautiful, these Anglo-Saxon types," the first man commented. "But Pedro Cortez' wife has not the looks of that girl, and she is too vivacious. That girl is quite... something!"

His wife looked down at the flashing rings on her hands, and her eyes flashed dangerous sparks.

"Don Carlos de Formera y Santos is not usually to be seen about with one of her type... whatever that type may be!" spitefully. "He is a man of taste and the utmost discretion, and is as good as engaged to the daughter of a retired English Ambassador who still lives in Seville. I have it on the very best authority that Sir James and Lady Hartingdon are quite delighted at the idea of the match, and the marriage is expected to be announced at any moment."

Both men looked at one another, and one lifted his eyebrows.

"In that case it certainly seems a little odd that..." And then he glanced again at April. "Although perhaps it isn't really odd," he murmured, *sotto voce*. "But it might have been wiser if he had not brought her to quite such a public place."

April was feeling that very strongly as she sensed the curiosity around her. She was not one of them, and they knew it, and Don Carlos was submitting her to an ordeal that was quite unnecessary. If he thought that he was providing her with some pleasurable entertainment then the pleasure was overlaid by the uneasiness she felt at being thrust into so much public notice in his company, and by her recollection of his remarks at lunch time. He had talked about her being compromised because they had been seen leaving the empty Cortez flat together ... Now that they were on full view in a night-club together, according to his codes every minute that passed she was being more seriously compromised, and as for him...!

Was he trying to convince her that he was perfectly serious when he proposed to her at lunch time?

She looked across the table at him a trifle agitatedly.

"Don Carlos," she said quickly, "I would like you to take me back to my hotel now, if—if you please..."

"The night is young," he said gravely, making no move to comply with her wish. "I had hoped you were having an enjoyable evening."

"I am," she assured him eagerly. "But I'm not used to the late hours you keep here in Spain, and—and I'm taking up a great deal of your time ..."

"Under the circumstances," he returned, "that is perfect nonsense. But if you are tired," with a sudden display of concern that filled her with considerable amazement, "I will most certainly take you back to your hotel. We will meet again for lunch tomorrow and have the talk that I was hoping we would have before we parted tonight ... or rather, this morning..."

"Is it as late as that?" with an aghast glance at her watch.

"It is nearly three o'clock."

"Then, Don Carlos, I must go." She could no

longer keep the agitation out of her face. "Don Carlos, earlier today you talked to me about..."

"I asked you to marry me."

"And of course I understood that you were merely being chivalrous. An Englishman wouldn't have considered for a moment that there was any necessity to be chivalrous just because... just because of a chain of circumstances in which he became involved. And anyone might have telephoned the flat at the time that you did, and anyone might have called..."

"That," Don Carlos told her, with a heavy frown between his brows, "is one reason why I find it hard to forgive Señor and Señora Cortez for placing you in the impossible situation that, through their complete lack of consideration, they did place you in. As you say, *anyone* might have called at the flat! And you were alone!"

Her eyes widened in astonishment.

"But I'm perfectly capable of looking after myself!"

"And your reputation?" he inquired.

"In England we don't bother as much about reputations as you do. I mean," as she saw him frown swiftly, and hoping she could correct a false impression, "we don't concern ourselves quite so much about people's reputations as you do here in Spain. We accept it that they are—what they appear to be!—and if something unfortunate happens to them we don't instantly think the worst."

She thought his whole expression grew a trifle bleak.

"In Spain we endeavour to protect our young women, but that quite obviously is what you do not do in England."

She could have pointed out to him that she hardly came under the category of " our young women," but there were other things that had to be made clear before they parted that night, and she decided not to waste any more time.

"*Señor*, before you take me back to the hotel——"

The same handsome, elderly woman who had bowed to Don Carlos at lunch time, while her demure-eyed daughter was with her, swept past in the company of several friends, on their way to a table, and Don Carlos stood up at once and almost pointedly greeted her and bowed over her hand.

"Allow me, *señora*," he said with much ceremony, "to present to you my fiancée, Miss April Day! April, my dear", turning to her with equal ceremony—and, even in the midst of her complete astonishment, April was aware of the way in which he said her name, with so much distinctness that it echoed in her ears for some time afterwards, and with a queer Spanish intonation that made it sound altogether different, somehow—"I would like you to meet my dear old friend, Señora Isabella Ribieros."

If Señora Ribieros was astounded by the introduction, April was completely taken aback. For one instant she was so uncertain that she had heard aright that she couldn't marshall her wits sufficiently to rise from her chair and acknowledge the Señora's aloof bow and jerkily spoken words of congratulation. And then, when she was on her feet, she had no idea whether to offer her hand, since the other made no attempt to offer hers, and the Spanish that she had acquired somewhat laboriously over the past few months fled from her as if she had never attempted to learn even a word.

"You are English, *señorita*?" the Señora said, coming to her aid and speaking awkward English even more jerkily.

April inclined her head, and was never afterwards in the least certain what she said beyond that. Or even whether she said anything at all that made sense to the other woman.

Señora Ribieros smiled bleakly at Don Carlos, and reminded him that he had English blood in his own veins. Was it not his maternal grandmother who was half English? Or was she wholly English?

"Wholly English, I believe, *señora*," Don Carlos returned, and of the three he was the only one who was completely calm and complacent, seeming slightly to enjoy the situation, as if his old friend's obvious perturbation—and it was very likely the demure daughter was not far from her thoughts—aroused an echo of amusement when it might have called for sympathy. "But that doesn't make me anything but extremely Spanish," he added, smiling with sudden devasting charm at both of them. "And although I am proud of my English blood, I'm afraid it was very watered down before it reached me."

"Not watered down," Señora Ribieros returned, with sudden spirit. "Possibly none of it reached you at all, otherwise you would not be so very Spanish. And," she emphasized, "it is a good thing to be very Spanish!"

She looked directly at April as if she could never possibly like her, and then remarked that no doubt they would be meeting frequently in the future, and she would await further news of the wedding with bated breath. Indeed, the news was so unexpected that it would enchant everybody—all Don Carlos's numberless friends!—and she had no doubt at all that his relatives were all greatly charmed.

"Especially your sister," she added, with a strange smirk of a smile. "I'm sure she is delighted."

"On the contrary, she knows nothing—as yet—about my plans," Don Carlos informed her smoothly. "Neither do any of my relatives. And you are the first of my friends, *señora*, to meet Miss Day."

"Is that so?" But her smile was beginning to wither her lips. "The privilege of a very old friend! I do appreciate it!" She bowed. "I mustn't keep you now. Young lovers are the same the world over, and delight in being alone. But you mustn't keep Miss Day from her chaperone too long, Carlos!" with an arch, cold look. "That would never do, when your fiancée is so obviously very young!" and she passed on and joined her friends in such a state of secret agitation that she could barely say a word when they spoke to her.

Don Carlos smiled to himself—as a newly engaged man has a right to smile—and then took April by her cool forearm and suggested that they leave.

"The ladies' cloakroom is at the head of the stairs if you wish to avail yourself of it. Although I believe you haven't a wrap to collect?"

"I haven't." She bit out the words, and then bit her lip. "Don Carlos, how dared you? I was about to tell you that I couldn't possibly marry you under any circumstances when Señora Ribieros came in——"

"And instead I told her we are betrothed to be married! It was an opportunity, and I seized it. By noon tomorrow the news will be all over Madrid!"

She looked suddenly almost frightened.

49

"But, Don Carlos," she whispered, "you know very well that it isn't true."

"Isn't it?" His fingers gripped her arm a little cruelly. "I do assure you, Miss Day—no, I mustn't say that! I must get used to the delightful name of April! —I do assure you that when I make an announcement I mean it! I was afraid you were not prepared to treat my proposal seriously, and as it was very serious, and I could not permit you to refuse me, I made it impossible for either of us to retreat. Whether you like it or not you are to become Señora Carlos de Formera y Santos in as short a time as arrangements can be made for our marriage."

She gasped.

"But you can't force me... you can't!"

His eyes gazed down coldly into hers.

"I said that we can neither of us retreat!"

CHAPTER V

AFTER that it seemed to April that some influence quite outside her own control had taken over the running and ordering of her life.

Although she would never have believed it, she found herself engaged to marry a man she knew little or nothing about, a man for whom she felt absolutely nothing save a kind of awe because he was so handsome and autocratic, with the power to impose his will on other people to the extent that they obeyed him when he insisted that something should be done. Even a young woman like herself, born and bred in freedom, and encouraged to use her will and think for herself from the time that she was considered old enough to go for walks by herself.

But now, because of some ridiculous idea about the conventions having been defied—Spanish conventions, at that!—she was to become the wife of a man who was no more interested in her than she was in him. Perhaps less interested, for whereas he had a certain power over her—he must have, since she wasn't laughing in his face and rushing off to her British Consulate for an assisted journey home—she had none whatsoever over him. Judging by the expression on his face whenever he looked at her he neither admired her nor approved of her. He had become involved with her through no fault of his own, and his peculiar Spanish conscience insisted that he put the matter right.

Although, looked at from the point of view of April, there was nothing to put right.

Then why did she allow him, from the moment that she met the bleak coldness of his eyes at nearly four o'clock in the morning, while they were still surrounded by all the over-opulent splendour of a Spanish night-club, and the lights were about to go down for yet another spell-binding performance by a couple of far-famed dancers, to wrest from her what little will she had left to oppose him and toss it carelessly away, as if it was a thing of no account? Why did she find it impossible to say a word as he guided her out into the night?

He took her back to her hotel, and told her he would be unable to see anything at all of her the following day, but the day after that he would telephone and prepare her for the hour at which he would call to take her out either to lunch or dinner, or merely for a short drive if he found himself too tied up with his engagements to spare her more time. He recommended her to enjoy herself placidly while he was unable to see anything of her, and if she wanted a car to take her on shopping expeditions, or for brief tours of Madrid, she had but to telephone the reception desk in the hotel and one would be round for her almost immediately.

"I don't know how much sight-seeing you have already done," he remarked, "but Madrid is a store-house of treasures for those who can appreciate them. Our churches, our museums, our art galleries, are all worth seeing. You need not be bored even for a moment if these things appeal to you."

"They do," she confessed, "but the thing that concerns me very much is ... how I'm going to pay

52

my hotel bill when the time comes! I'm so terribly afraid it's going to be much, much more than I can afford!"

Instantly she felt the freezing coldness of his disapproval.

"We will hear no more about your hotel bill, if you please, *mia cara*," he requested her, while she wondered whether there were many men in Spain who were as tall and as impressive as he was ... particularly in a white dinner jacket with a gardenia in the buttonhole. "That is something that no longer concerns you, and my affair entirely. You are not to worry about financial matters of any sort." He paused. "I have paid into your bank the sum of money that was owing to you from Señor Cortez. If you want anything further you have but to ask for it."

She reached frantically for her independence, and tried hard to hold on to it.

"I will pay you back," she assured him, "if ... if I have to touch it!"

He smiled. She wasn't at all certain that she liked the smile, although it revealed his beautiful, hard white teeth, and was rather more amused than most of his smiles.

"You forget," he reminded her, "that in a short while there will be no necessity for you to even think of paying me back. I shall be your husband!"

The next morning flowers were delivered to her suite, and although they were not the offerings of a lover—flesh-pink carnations and roses, so delicate, so exquisitely scented that their perfume was soon filling the room—she gathered them up in her arms when she had lifted them from their box and held them against her face, and for one moment she was almost completely overwhelmed by the unexpectedness of the gift.

But that didn't prevent her haunting the air-line offices that morning, and several times she stepped forward to address one of the clerks behind the polished counter, and request a vacant seat on an early flight to England. There was enough money in the bank to cover her fare—actually far more than that—and she could do as she had said she would do and pay Don Carlos back as soon as she got back to her own country. There was the tiny sum deposited in an English bank, which was all that her father had been able to leave her, which she could draw upon when the necessity arose, and there must be some means of overcoming currency difficulties and getting the money back to Spain and the man who had lent it to her. Although she knew that he refused to regard it as a loan.

But every time she stepped forward someone got between her and the counter, and suddenly she found herself confronting the mental image of Don Carlos, and seeing that strange, forbidding look in his eyes— that look which challenged her—as he said, as if she no longer had the smallest option to pursue her own road through life, without finding it necessary to devote at least an occasional thought to him:

"I have said that we can neither of us retreat!"

If she took his money and flew home to England she would leave him with a lot of explaining to do to his friends. *She* would have compromised him and walked out on him, a proud man who wouldn't find it an enjoyable situation to be walked out on! He was depending on her not to let that situation arise.

She found herself making her way out into the blinding hot sunshine of Madrid and feeling as if a net had closed round her. She was no longer, however much she tried to assure herself that she was, a free agent. The Cortez family quarrel had recoiled on her in a way she could never have imagined that it would recoil on her!

That evening Don Carlos dropped in on her at the cocktail hour, although he had said she would see nothing of him that day, and he presented her with a breathtakingly beautiful ring that exactly fitted her finger, although he had had no guide at all to the size of it.

It was a large milky pearl mounted in a claw of platinum and diamonds, and when April first saw it it was lying on a bed of velvet in a satin-lined case. The sheer loveliness of it widened her eyes, and she could say nothing at all for several seconds. Then she ejaculated, "Oh, how beautiful!" and Don Carlos reached for her hand and slipped it on to her finger.

"It fits?" he inquired, as if he had no doubt at all that it would fit.

"Perfectly." Then she looked up at him, and concern filled her face. "But you don't mean that it's for me? That I'm to wear it?"

"But of course." That coldly amused smile curved his lips. "It is usual, when a betrothal takes place, for the prospective bridegroom to place a ring upon the finger of his prospective bride. Even in England I believe that is the custom, is it not?"

She nodded dumbly.

"Well, then, why do you look so amazed?"

"I—I hadn't realized that you would be giving me a

ring. I—I can't really believe that I'm engaged to you!"

He studied her with a curious intentness, and yet at the same time there was a faintly whimsical gleam in his eyes, and it added a little upward quirk to the corners of his lips.

"Shall I tell you something?" he said.

She nodded, her own eyes very large and golden as she gazed at him, and just a little cloudy, as the result of her mixed emotions, rather like cloudy amber.

From her he glanced swiftly round her room... and, somewhat to her surprise, he had ascended to her sitting-room today.

"I see you have made the most of the flowers I sent you," he said, noticing how beautifully she had arranged them in bowls and vases. "But I will be honest with you and admit that I was fully prepared to find that you were no longer here when I arrived this afternoon. I expected to find a polite little note awaiting me, informing me that you had seized the opportunity to fly home. I even telephoned the airline company's offices this morning to inquire whether a young Englishwoman named Day had booked a seat on one of the earliest flights that would leave Madrid."

"You... did?"

"Yes." His eyes were infinitely dark as they met and held hers, but they were still smiling. "Are you going to tell me that it never once occurred to you that now was your chance to break away from me for ever? I would not have come after you, you know! And in England you would have been able to laugh at me and my stupid Spanish ideas of what is done, and what is not done!"

"I... I'm quite sure your ideas are not stupid," But

she was forced to lower her eyes before the probing, searching quality in his regard, and a guilty conscience sent a revealing food of delicate colour stealing up into her cheeks. "But it's perfectly true I did make an early call at the airline offices, and I did fully intend—when I arrived there!—to buy myself a ticket back to England. You had placed a sum of money for me in the bank, and I ... I thought I could pay you back."

"Then why didn't you do so? Why didn't you buy your ticket to England?" he asked her. "What stopped you?"

"Nothing ... At least, I don't quite know what stopped me ..."

"But you came out without a ticket, and you came back here to await the moment when I would get in contact with you again?"

"Yes."

"Ah!" he exclaimed, and let out a strange sound like a sigh, and also partly like a long-drawn-out murmur of incredulity. "I find that interesting! I also find it almost unbelievable."

He walked across to a vase of carnations, and snapped one off and attached it to his buttonhole. He was gazing down at it admiringly when he spoke to her again.

"I think you told me that your father was a clergyman, Miss Day," he said. "And only this morning the clergyman's daughter could not bear to let me down! She thought more of the embarrassment of the situation I would be in than her own urgent desire to get away back to her own country. Nothing else that you could have done or said, Miss Day—April!" walking back to her, "could have so convinced me that I am a lucky man to have met you. Perhaps a very lucky man!"

His eyes were alive and bright with interest as he gazed at her, and she felt her pulses quicken absurdly, as if a half-hearted race that she had been running had developed suddenly into an important effort. She felt her cheeks begin to burn under the strange brilliance of his eyes, and, partly to cover her confusion, and partly because she wanted to know the answer, she said:

"Will you tell me something else, *señor*? Apart from your sense of chivalry, and the extraordinary belief that you seem to hold that you owe me the opportunity to marry you in order to remain respectable, is there some other reason why you yourself were not entirely appalled by the thought of marrying a young woman you knew little or nothing about? Did I, perhaps, 'happen' to you at just the right moment?"

"Your phraseology is a little strange," he told her, "but the unequivocal answer is yes! You 'happened' to me at a moment when I had problems of my own, and it seemed to me that you might solve those problems." He took her hand and lifted it, and gazed at his ring intently. "I would prefer not to discuss those problems with you if you do not mind, but I would also like you to know that this arrangement we have entered into is not entirely one-sided. Where you are concerned, I can give you security, promise that you will be well taken care of for the rest of your life, and that no future Señor and Señora Cortez will ever be able to plunge you into difficulties. And, where I am concerned, you can take your place at my side as a wife. I am rather badly in need of, to entertain my friends, transform the several houses I own into homes where it is pleasant to reside, and lend a little colour to my existence. Does that make sense to you?"

This time it was she who let out a sound that was half sigh of relief, half sheer incredulity.

"It makes more sense," she admitted.

"And in time we will get to know one another, and then you will not feel that it is all too bizarre for words. You might even cease to credit me with the remarkably chivalrous qualities you credit me with at the present time, and in you I might discover a companion for the years that lie ahead who could not have been bettered had I had all the world to choose from." His eyes were mocking, but when he carried her hand up to his lips and kissed it the touch of his mouth had the queerest and most unexpected effect on her. She felt as if every nerve in her body tingled, and she was quite unprepared for such an experience. "So will you now look upon our engagements not as something that has been forced upon us, but as something remarkably fortuitous which we may live to be very happy about?"

"I—I'll try," she said, but even so she could not really believe that he meant to marry her, and that, with the placing of his ring on her finger, she was committed to marry him. She looked down at the ring, and was bemused by the size and quality of the pearl. "How—how did you manage to guess my size so accurately?" she asked.

He smiled.

"You have very small hands, very lovely hands ... I wouldn't have been a man if it hadn't struck me how unusually lovely they are! Quite unsuited to performing menial tasks for Señora Cortez and her offspring. And, of course, if the ring had not fitted I would have had it altered."

He bent once more and brushed his lips lightly against the tips of her fingers.

"And now I think you might enjoy a short drive before sunset," he said. "There is a full hour yet before it will be dark, and already the atmosphere is cooling."

They drove slowly along the fragrant avenues, growing noisy with the crowds who were pouring into them from shops and offices, out to where the Royal Palace stands upon a rocky eminence and is surrounded by a noble park of pine and eucalyptus trees. From there April could look across to the sierra and see the snow that lies there glinting in the changing light of sunset, and on their way back the whole of Madrid was bathed in a lovely pinkish-mauve light like the petals of the Judas trees that rain gently upon the heads of customers frequenting the open-air cafés on the Recoletos.

April found the courage to ask Don Carlos shyly:

"Do you live in Madrid, *señor*?" It seemed an extraordinary question once she had asked it, for he obviously must have some place of residence in the capital, and it was the more extraordinary since it might one day be her own place of residence as well. "I mean, have you a house here?"

"Yes," he answered, driving very carefully in the confusing light. "I have a house here, but it is at the moment undergoing extensive alterations, and is not really habitable at the present time. For the past few weeks I have been living at my club."

"I see," she murmured.

He glanced at her for a moment sideways.

"One day I will take you to see my house. But tomorrow I am flying to Majorca, where I have a fruit and flower farm which, also you must see one day, and when I return I plan to take you south to Seville. I will place you in the care of my sister, who will be a very adequate chaperone for you until our marriage can be arranged."

It sounded quite fantastic . . . *Until our marriage can be arranged*. But it was the mention of his sister, and that "very adequate chaperone," that destroyed her mood of near-complacence. She couldn't tell why, but they aroused a hollow, uneasy feeling inside her, and even after several seconds that hollowness remained. And the formal little speech went on echoing in her ears.

"I know nothing about you," she said suddenly, uneasiness in her voice. "I don't even know about the members of your family!"

He smiled, but this time he did not glance round at her. He was concentrating on the road ahead.

"You will meet them all in time," he said.

CHAPTER VI

THEY arrived in Seville about a week later. During that week April had had so much spare time on her hands, experienced so many emotions that were new to her, and resisted so many impulses to forget that she was, after all, a clergyman's daughter, and put a period to this extraordinary interlude in her life, that she felt completely unlike herself and was not at all sure that she was capable of appreciating this glimpse of an entirely different Spain.

At least, that was the way she felt during the journey, when Don Carlos was overwhelming her with polite attentions, and yet seemed spiritually miles removed from her at the same time. She was not accustomed to travelling by air, and she was secretly nervous, but he sensed it and distracted her attention with pleasant conversation before they took off, and afterwards he continued the conversation until she was more relaxed, and fell silent when she wished he would go on talking to her about Majorca and the island's flowers, about his villa beside the sea and the peach groves he had so recently been inspecting.

He had a voice which she found almost soothing to listen to, carefully modulated, the diction smooth and precise, and his very faint accent when he spoke English intrigued her. She found herself waiting for the moments when he spoke her name, seeming to linger over it for an unnecessary second or so, and when he called her *"mia cara."* There was nothing in being called "my dear" by the man you were to marry, but when the man was as elusive, as unreal, as picturesque as Don Carlos de Formera y Santos, and when she couldn't believe even for a moment that she would ever marry him, it was vaguely exciting to be thus addressed.

And once—he probably didn't realize what he was saying, she thought afterwards—he called her *"amada,"* and took possession of her nervous, fluttering hand when their seat belts were fastened, and she was feeling rather sick.

Instantly the sickness passed, and she was able to appreciate that swift climb into the brazen blue above Madrid, and the golden sunshine that—although it was also uncomfortably hot—flooded all around them.

But by the time they arrived in Seville he had grown quiet and remote... almost as remote, if not quite as icily cold, as when she first met him.

Seville was just coming to life after the heat of the day, and the lamp standards were already lit and shining like stars amongst the greenery of palms. Hundreds of other wrought-iron lanterns sent out pale beams in quiet *patios,* and ornamental gateways had a light shining above them. The narrow streets that open into squares full of rustling foliage were pinpricked here and there with light, and growing intensely black in the shadows.

April caught the eternal scent of flowers floating on the warm air, and as she and Don Carlos tunnelled deep into the heart of all this light and shadow in a big, black, glistening car that had met them at the airport—Don Carlos's cream car had been left behind in Madrid—she remembered that this was Andalusia, the land of flowers and gardens overflowing with colour, just as every balcony was draped with it, and every trellis had its climbing rose.

On the back seat of the car, sharing it with her, Don Carlos said nothing as they tunnelled deeper into the heart of the city. Although he was so close to her that she could have put out a hand and touched him April had the feeling that he was far removed from her in spirit.

Something was preoccupying him to an abnormal extent. She wondered whether it was the thought of his sister, and possibly other members of his family —since he had not denied that he had a family—and the way they would react when he presented to them his future bride. Someone they had never even heard of before!

The car was chauffeur-driven, and if anything else was needed to convince the English girl that he was a man of wealth and substance, the subservience of the chauffeur would have convinced her. He was even dressed in livery, and the interior of the car was so luxurious that April felt positively lapped about by it, as if she was travelling on a cloud of opulence and ease.

In a remarkably short time she realized that they had left the city and its outskirts behind them, and were heading into the country. It was by now quite dark, and although she could see stars shining up in the violet-blue sky, and the golden crescent of a young moon hung like a brooch in the same unclouded immensity, she could make out little or nothing else. She had an impression of openness and space, of the sky hanging low above the earth, and in through the open windows of the car came the salt breath of the sea.

Don Carlos spoke at last.

"We will soon be there."

April said nothing at all.

He put out a hand and touched her lightly, as if to make certain she was still there beside him.

"You are tired, *cara*?"

"Not really." How could she tell him that she was full of uneasy forebodings, that the thought of meeting possibly, a mother as well—filled her with near panic? The only Spanish people she had ever lived with were Señor and Señora Cortez, and Señora Cortez had been no more Spanish than she was. She had run her home on free-and-easy American lines and atmosphere had been altogether free of formality. But one could not expect the mother and sister of a man like Don Carlos de Formera y Santos to be free of formality. Almost certainly they would be frighteningly stiff—paralysingly stiff was a better word, for excessive good manners and an overpowering belief in correctness have the effect of freezing the blood in the veins of a more impulsive person. Or so April herself had found.

She lay back against the yielding upholstery of the car, and to her surprise Don Carlos touched her again. Only this time he took possession of her hand.

"What is it?" he asked. "What is troubling you, April?"

She swallowed on the nervous lump in her throat.

"Your sister," she managed. "I've been thinking... I'm a complete stranger to her, and why should she put herself out to receive me, to have me in her house?"

"It is my house," he corrected her quietly.

She felt a slight sensation of relief.

65

"But even so ... what will you tell her about us? Will you tell her the truth, that we hardly know one another?"

"I shall tell her nothing beyond the fact that we are to be married," he replied quietly. "And, as a matter of fact, so much she already knows."

"You have ... written to her?"

"I have been in touch with her."

The car travelled another half mile, and then she asked through the uneasy darkness:

"Is your sister married?"

"No."

After that she attempted nothing further in the way of conversation, and they swept between a pair of entrance gates and up a short dark drive to a house that shone startlingly white in the starshine. April could make out no actual details, but she had an impression of a courtyard with white buildings ranged on four sides of it, and a wide arch beneath which they disappeared to reappear in the middle of the courtyard.

A door opened, and a flood of golden light cut like a golden swordblade across the courtyard. As she stepped from the car April saw dark red roses growing in ordered beds close to the house, and roses wreathed the white columns of the verandas which the light refused to penetrate. Before the dark figure appeared in the entrance and held out its hand to her she cast a swift glance at the usual star-like lanterns which hung at the various angles of the courtyard, as well as above the entrance arch, and thought that they looked like jewels against the velvety night sky.

But the figure waiting to receive her spoke stiffly.

"You are tired, *señorita*? You have had a long journey from Madrid!"

"Not really long, as distances go nowadays," April heard herself answering, with the jerkiness she found it impossible to overcome when she was feeling really nervous, and felt her hand clasped for an instant by a cool, beringed one. Then the figure, dressed in black, with many underskirts that rustled, stepped backwards into the shadows of the hall to permit her to enter.

"Ah, Carlos, how very good to see you!"

It swept forward again to embrace the tall figure of Don Carlos, and although it was only in a vague way that she noticed these things, April saw the thin white arms go round his neck, the severe black head bend backwards a little while the dark eyes peered at him, and Don Carlos answered in a tone of voice that was much softer than anything she herself had yet heard from him:

"And it is good to see you, Ignatia!"

She let her hands fall from his neck and smiled at him, withdrawing with that graceful, rustling movement that was like the rustling of leaves in a light wind. They were together in the middle of a square of carpet that was full of rich blues and reds, and the light from the swinging lantern above them bathed them in a flood of amber.

"All is well with you, *cara*?" he asked. "Everything is well here?"

"Quite well," she replied, and then turned once more to April. "But you have not yet presented your fiancée to me ... not formally," she rebuked him gently.

He did so, taking April by the hand.

"Miss April Day, and you will, of course, call her April! April, this is my sister, Doña Ignatia. She looks after my home and runs everything for me."

Sinister words, if April had been a normal bride he was presenting, with dreams of running her own home without assistance from anyone save the servants. For Doña Ignatia had the look of a woman who could run a home perfectly, was accustomed to every aspect of housekeeping and capable of coping with every difficulty; and in addition there was something about her that suggested she had been born for that one purpose, and proposed to go on doing so for the rest of her life. She had dark eyes that were probably even more inscrutable than her brother's—full of wisdom, but unlikely to impart it to anyone else—a smooth, pale mask of a face, and the thin figure of a born spinster. She was probably a little older than her brother, without his somewhat startling good looks, and no doubt that was one reason why she was a spinster.

April sent a wondering, admiring glance around the hall, and—not being a normal bride-to-be—merely envied her her ability to get the very best out of her servants, for every solid piece of black oak furniture shone, every rug was jewel-bright. And although there were few feminine touches—an entire absence of flowers—the hall was beautiful.

"Your letter was so brief, Carlos, and there was so little time," her gentle voice protested yet again. "But, even so, we have prepared a room for Miss Day, and a sitting-room adjoining. She should be quite comfortable."

"I am sure she will be very comfortable," Carlos

returned soothingly. He started to look about him, glancing upwards at the staircase, and the gallery that ran above it. "But where is Constancia? I fully expected that she would be waiting to greet us!"

"Constancia is in her room," Doña Ignatia informed him, looking down at her white hands. "The child has a touch of the headache."

"Impossible!" Don Carlos declared, looking amazed. "I have never known Constancia to suffer with a headache in her life!" he frowned. What is wrong? Why is she keeping to her room?"

His sister shrugged her shoulders slightly, without looking up.

"The child is perhaps unhappy. I do not know," she murmured, and then summoned a servant to take April's luggage to the rooms prepared for her. "Juan, carry these cases upstairs, and then come back for the trunk." She looked full into her brother's eyes. "Your letter, as I have said, was brief... and it was also sudden. Constancia was not prepared for it."

"What do you mean?" he demanded coldly.

Again the shrug.

"That is all I can tell you. The rest I must leave to your imagination! No doubt in the morning she will be more resigned, and you will see her then. I would not, if I were you, disturb her tonight."

But, from the expression on Don Carlos's face, this was an eventuality he had not expected to have to cope with, and it was plain that he was annoyed... intensely annoyed. April had seen him frown before, and she had seen his eyes glitter with icy displeasure, but never as they glittered now, as if something that mattered to him very much indeed had recoiled on him, and had to be dealt with. His jaw set grimly, and he made for the stairs.

"This is a matter that cannot wait until morning," he said, and then glanced up and saw the girl coming slowly down the wide staircase towards him. She was young and dark and sullen, and as beautiful as a damask rose with the dew on it. The simile did not occur to April then, but it occurred to her afterwards. And it also occurred to her that, for one who was so beautiful, and should have been absolutely sure of herself, she almost cringed, and looked apprehensive, although her eyes were filled with resentment.

"Ah!" Don Carlos exclaimed, with deadly coldness, as he watched her descent. "So you are no longer suffering from the headache, Constancia?"

The girl's eyes filled with tears, and her voluptuous scarlet mouth quivered. She looked as if she had spent the entire afternoon weeping stormily, and her eyes were red from her weeping. Her body shrank as she drew near the waiting man, and the childish lines of her figure were plainly revealed through the sober dark material of her dress.

Then, as if she was a spring released, she hurled herself upon him, beat at him with frenzied fists, and burst into a positive torrent of tears and sobs. Don Carlos caught both of her wrists and fastidiously held her away from the front of his immaculate suit, and as he looked down at her his face was so harsh that April, behind them, felt an upsurge of deepest pity for the girl.

"Enough!" Don Carlos said, his voice still icy. "Enough, I say, Constancia!" His fingers on her wrists made red marks which were revealed when she snatched one of them free. "What is the meaning of this scene? Why are you behaving like this, when I expected you would be waiting to welcome Señorita Day and myself?"

"Señorita Day? But she is English!..." Constancia snatched free her other wrist, and then turned to confront April. Through the tears that were still coursing their way down her cheeks and hanging on her lashes like bright jewels her eyes blazed with resentment, and the fiercest dislike. "She is English, and you are going to marry her!" A stream of Spanish that was utterly incomprehensible to the English listener poured from her lips, and she ended with: "Oh, Carlos, *mi amado,* how can you? I warn you I will hate her always!... *always!*"

It might have been the effect of the light, but April thought Don Carlos looked suddenly pale as well as grim.

"You are talking like a ridiculous child," he said.

"I am not, I am not!" she declared. Abruptly she hurled herself upon him again, clutching at him. "And that is another mistake you make, for I am no longer a child. You persist in treating me as if I am, but I am a woman... not a child!" Tears gushed from her eyes again, and she wept more desolately. "It is bad enough that you marry, but that you treat me like a child... that is something I can't endure!" and she buried her face in his neck and proceeded to soak his immaculate flowing tie.

A good deal of the harshness died out of his face, and he stroked her tumbled mane of hair.

"Come, *amada,*" he said, more softly, "you are being absurd. I think of you as Constancia, and it is as Constancia that I wish to present you to Miss Day.

71

Cease ruining my tie, and dry your eyes, and tell her how much you regret this unpleasant scene."

"But I don't," Constancia said mutinously, without lifting her head.

From several feet away Doña Ignatia spoke quietly.

"Do as my brother requests, Constancia!"

The girl obeyed, not exactly with alacrity, but she certainly obeyed. For the second time she stepped backwards, drove her knuckles into her eyes, and glared at April.

"I regret the unpleasant scene, *señorita*! I also regret my rudeness, for I am sixteen, and should have better manners."

"You should, indeed," Don Carlos agreed, and then laughed suddenly and caught her by her hair and tugged her towards him. "But it is something that you have apologized, and I forgive you, and I'm sure Miss Day forgives you, too. Offer her your hand, and welcome her in a polite Spanish fashion."

But before he let her go he stroked her cheek, ruffled her hair, and then watched critically as she offered her hand to April. The latter took it and clasped it, hot and sticky though it was, warmly.

"You have nothing to apologize to me for," she said. "I'm afraid you had insufficient warning of my coming."

Constancia's expression grew only a little less hostile, and Don Carlos seized the opportunity to explain to his bride-to-be:

"This is my adopted daughter, Constancia. She is not usually so difficult to handle, and today we will hope is an exception."

But a perfectly understandable exception, April

thought, as she saw the sudden tremble of Constancia's lower lip, and the quiver of her chin. The girl —and, being Spanish, she certainly was not any longer a child!—was in love with her adoptive parent, and, whether he realized it or not; it was a wild and stormy and possessive love that could hardly be expected to diminish just because he had elected to take a wife.

As if the scene had affected Doña Ignatia's sense of the fitness of things more acutely than it had done that of anyone else, she once more spoke from the foot of the stairs, and her lips were tight.

"If you will be so good as to come this way, Miss Day, I will show you to your rooms."

The rest of that evening passed in a distinctly unreal fashion for April. After feeling slightly depressed by her two adjoining rooms and bathroom—which were magnificent without being strictly comfortable or the sort of rooms in which one could relax—she dressed in something white and plain for dinner, and then went down to find Doña Ignatia looking perfectly splendid in black satin and diamonds, and Constancia more simply but exquisitely attired in black lace, with a white flower in her hair.

That hair had undergone a beautifying process that was quite startling, and it shone like satin—blackish-bronze satin—under the lights in the immensely formal dining *sala*. It was very obvious that both of the female members of Don Carlos's household had gone to great pains to appear at their best in honour of the arrival of Don Carlos's fiancée, and although April looked charming—and very English—in her simple white, she wished she had selected something just a little more in keeping with the elaborate appearance tof the other two.

After dinner they all sat in the big main *sala* and sipped coffee which was dispensed by Doña Ignatia, who looked a very fitting chatelaine of such a house presiding over the fragile cups and the handsome silver tray and coffee-pot, etc. And then Don Carlos was called away to interview an unexpected caller, the ladies produced needlework—or rather, Doña Ignatia did; Constancia sat with her hands tightly locked together in her lap, her eyes, black, brooding and beautiful, fixed on April's face as if it had for her an irresistible attraction. The white flower in her hair was of the same creamy whiteness as her skin, and although she was only sixteen her brilliant mouth had the sultry seductiveness of the mouth of a far older woman.

At last Doña Ignatia suggested to her that she play the piano, and she performed expertly on a very fine instrument. The music was formal and carefully chosen, and as it drifted out through the open windows into the warmth of the Spanish night April thought it must have a slightly alien sound. But it convinced her—as was no doubt intended—that Constancia had been well brought up, and had received the usual number of advantages of young girls of her class, in spite of the bad impression she might have created as a result of her stormy outburst earlier in the evening.

It was only when she grew tired of playing the piano and lifted a guitar off the wall and started to play it that April was able to feel she was listening to the real Constancia. Her eyes were dreamy, and her mouth curved upwards excitingly with her dreams, and she forgot the presence of the other two.

She was in a world of her own, lost, contemplative, happy. But it was not an entirely satisfying happiness, for her eyes still brooded. April, who had seen them bright with tears and blazing with a kind of temporary hate, wondered how they would look when the girl was in love. When, that was, she was able to reveal her love.

Doña Ignatia frowned over her needlework, and when the soft strumming had gone on for little more than ten minutes she ordered the girl, curtly, to put the instrument away and go to bed.

But, upstairs in her room, April continued to hear it for a long while, and she thought it was far more in keeping with the purple magic of the night than Chopin. Chopin in an English drawing-room was one thing, but here in the heart of Andalusia it was another. And Constancia's fingers awakened a wild, unexplainable longing that was probably the secret longing in her own heart.

April sat beside her window, not feeling any urge to get undressed and go to bed, and she recalled the look of Don Carlos when his anger had passed and he was anxious only to soothe his ward. To win her back to good humour.

His fingers had been very gentle as they stroked her hair, his voice almost wooingly kind. And for a very fastidious man he had not complained overmuch about his ruined tie.

He was almost certainly very fond of Constancia, startled by her unexpected attitude. And, after being called away, he had not returned to say good night to his fiancée. April had sat on and on in the *sala*, listening for his footsteps, and it was only when Doña Ignatia indicated that she was about to retire that the realization swept over her that she was faced with no other alternative but to retire, too.

Without saying good night to Don Carlos.

As she went up the heavily carved staircase to her room she felt as if she had been deprived of something.

CHAPTER VII

In the morning she awakened to wonder where she was, and when she saw the golden bars of sunlight finding their way in through her closed shutters she sprang out of bed to open them.

Outside her windows lay all the loveliness of an Andalusian morning. Already a brilliant arc of blue sky swept without a sign of cloud overhead, and in the distance she could see the sea, blue—or even bluer—than the sky. Immediately underneath the window, which had a green-painted balcony outside it, and on which she stood to enjoy all the freshness of the morning, there was a green lawn that sparkled wetly from the recent hosing it had received by gardeners, and a long line of rose pergolas was also bright with diamond drops that had not yet evaporated in the heat of the sun.

As far as she could see the country round about was flat, extending in a somewhat barren fashion to the sea. Inland it was probably mountainous. The diaphanous quality of the light was something that fascinated her, and she found it hard to recall the heavy purple dusk that had pressed upon everything the evening before. Don Carlos's house, in the daylight, was a revelation too, for it went spreading in all directions, although most of it was built round the central courtyard, and it was white and gracious, with pan-tiled roofs that were rosy as apricots.

April dressed herself quickly in powder blue and went down into the garden to see whether there was anyone about apart from herself. It was quite early yet, but she had an idea this was not a sluggish household, and in Spain most people are early risers, even if they go to bed at extraordinary hours, for the heat of the day makes it impossible for anyone to do very much work, and the only real coolness while summer lasts is to be found in the early mornings.

And, while she was on her balcony, April thought she caught a glimpse of someone astride a horse flash past like a figment of imagination. If it was actually an early morning rider he was gone in an instant, but April would have been prepared to swear that he had a pillion rider, and that pillion rider was wearing something gay and scarlet. And she had laughed . . . Her laughter had come floating along on the wind until it reached April's balcony.

That was one reason why she had hurried with her dressing. If it was Don Carlos who was indulging in his favourite form of early morning exercise, then she might catch yet another glimpse of him when he returned to hand over his mount.

The stables were at the back of the house, forming four sides of yet another courtyard, but there was no sign of any life when April drew near. Human life, that is, for one or two of the half-doors were open, and she could see some splendid examples of horse-flesh noisily enjoying their breakfasts as she stood watching them for several minutes. And there was a sound of washing down, and a tuneless whistling which, apparently is indulged in by stable lads in other corners of the world as well as England. Or that was the thought which passed through April's mind.

And then, as she was preparing to turn away, she heard the unmistakable clatter of hooves, and round an angle of the buildings came the same horse that she had only momentarily glimpsed before—and she knew now that she was right; it was a bright chestnut, with a flowing, undocked tail—and on its back was Don Carlos, and perched in a pillion behind Don Carlos was the girl he looked upon as an adopted daughter, the lovely Constancia, who was so infinitely more than just lovely this morning that April stood quite still and stared up at her.

Hair once more loose, and streaming out behind her, she had a colour like a rose, and was clinging with honey-coloured, slim bare arms to her guardian's waist. She was wearing a short, vivid skirt of scarlet, and about her neck was a scarlet bandanna, tied in a careless knot. As soon as they came to a standstill she jumped clear of her perch without any assistance from anyone, and by the time Don Carlos alighted she was greeting April with a brilliant smile and sparkling eyes, and chattering away to her in moderately good English without any inhibitions of any kind, and absolutely no sign of hostility.

"You slept well, *señorita*? You look as if you slept very well indeed, you are so golden and charming." She caught hold of her guardian's arm, and leaned against him as she gazed up into his face. "Is not Miss Day quite typical of England? So pale and delicate, like a spring morning, and as uncertain as the sunshine!"

He tweaked her ear.

"A lot you know about England, *chiquita*. You spent a few weeks there once, when you were very young, but that is all." Then he turned to April and smiled at her in his somewhat heart-jolting fashion. In addition his eyes studied her carefully. "If I may be permitted to say so, you do indeed resemble sunshine, *mia cara*," he told her. His eyes were on her shining hair, swinging, as always, loose on her shoulders, and as her eyelids fluttered, and she looked straight up at him, he found himself looking deep into her extraordinarily limpid golden-brown eyes. The increasing heat was warming her skin, and it was golden, also—but a paler gold than Constancia's.

Constancia, at sixteen—actually, April discovered later, she was close upon seventeen—was a full-blown rose, like the scarlet rose she wore behind one ear. But April, at twenty-four, was a mere pale bud, a half-opened yellow rose of the type that often has to be nursed along in a hothouse.

Not that she was really delicate, but she had none of the robust constitution of Constancia. Although born and brought up in the country she was a little afraid of trampling horses' hooves too, and she moved backwards somewhat hurriedly as Don Carlos's spirited chestnut, its desire for exercise only partially abated by the quick run it had been given that morning, reared unexpectedly on to its hind legs and was handed over by Don Carlos to a groom.

He gave the mare a pat, and then moved to the side of April. He drew her out of the path of the trampling hooves, and then bent and kissed her hand.

"That is to wish you good morning," he said, with strange softness, as he once more smiled into her eyes. "I must offer you my apologies for last night, and my omission to say good night to you. But I was called away, and by the time I returned you had gone to bed."

She felt almost as if her heart lifted. A faint but unmistakable depression, with which she had awakened—and which she had refused to believe was due to that omission of the night before—floated magically away from her, and, overwhelmingly aware of the fact that he was still holding her hand (was there something electric about the touch of his fingers? she wondered. Something that set her own fingers tingling?) she coloured as if she had been caught off her guard, and assured him at once:

"Oh, I quite understood! And, as a matter of fact, I think I went to bed rather early."

"By Madrid standards, you mean?" He was still smiling, a little quizzically. "Here we do not attempt to turn night into day."

He was wearing a hard Spanish hat, that was fastened beneath his attractive bronzed chin with a strap, and in his Spanish-style riding dress, with polished boots and glittering spurs, he had the odd effect of making her heart not merely lift, but turn over. It occurred to her to wonder, like a thought out of the blue, what she had done to merit this transition from a working life—a life of looking after a small child, and attending to all his daily needs—to the unreal existence of a publicly acclaimed fiancée of such a man as this, who could be disturbing, magnetically attractive when he felt like it.

And she had a vague suspicion that he felt like it this morning.

Constancia, patting the chestnut before it was led away, and feeding it lumps of sugar, looked sideways over her shoulder at them, and a little of her exuberant good humour seemed to fade from her eyes.

"You are not too fond of horses, Miss Day?" she inquired, an apparent quirk of mischief at the corner of her mouth. "You do not care to come too close and

reward this beauty as I do, with a lump of sugar?"
She threw an arm about the satin-smooth neck. "See,
nothing could be more docile!"

But when, as if in response to a challenge, April
would have conquered her nervousness and stepped
forward, Don Carlos gripped her by the arm, and
spoke sharply.

"Do not allow that naughty one to goad you, *chiquita*!" he cautioned her. " She fears nothing and no
one ... not even me!" a trifle grimly. "And she was
born on the back of a horse ... or the next best thing
to it, for her mother was a great rider!"

"I see," April murmured, and wondered why she
had felt so strongly compelled to defy that taunt in the
glittering dark eyes of the born rider, who was also so
very beautiful.

Constancia pouted at him, and tossed the chestnut's
reins to the waiting groom.

"You do not tell me enough about my mother, Carlos," she protested.

He frowned swiftly.

"You have far too insatiable a curiosity," he rebuked her. "Now, run away, and dress yourself in
something more suitable than that abbreviated skirt.
And how many more times must I tell you that I do
not approve of that careless hair style?"

She pouted again, but she also peeped at him co-
quettishly between her thick eyelashes.

"Rodrigo tells me that it suits me," she told him.

"Rodrigo is nothing but a boy," he snapped. "A
mere callow youth! Now, do as I tell you, and have
less to say for yourself!"

But she had one thing more to say.

"I will if you will promise to take me riding again

tomorrow morning," she pleaded. Her eyes were soft, appealing as a doe's, big and black as the night. "Please, Carlos!"

April could almost feel his resistance seeping out of him as he stood looking down at her from his infinitely superior height, and she could sense the indulgence that took its place even before he uttered a word in response to her plea. And when it came, that word was the word Constancia wanted, unconditional agreement, although from the rueful look on his mouth it was wrung out of him by nothing less than her one hundred per cent feminine appeal, and the affection he had for her.

"Yes. Since you will pester me all day if I refuse."

But the qualification meant nothing, April realized. And Constancia let out a little delighted cry, clapped her hands, blew him an unashamed kiss, and then fled round a corner of the buildings.

April looked upwards at Don Carlos.

"You find it difficult to refuse her anything, don't you?" she said quietly.

When he looked down at her his eyes were dark and unrevealing, as if a screen had come down over them.

"Perhaps," he agreed. "But she is very young, and very endearing."

"She is also beautiful," she said.

He thought for a moment, and then agreed with her emphatically.

"Very beautiful! But her mother was even more beautiful." They were walking back to the house, and he had placed his hand beneath her elbow to ensure that she took the right path. "Shall I tell you about her?" he asked abruptly.

April felt her heart start to beat quickly, uncomfortably quickly, but she answered composedly:

"Yes, please do, if . . . if you feel that you would like to do so."

Although she wasn't looking at him, she knew he was frowning hard at the path as they walked.

"She and I were betrothed to be married, but she married someone else ... I was eighteen, and she was several years older. When Constancia was born her health was not at all good, and by the time Constancia was five it had deteriorated so badly that we all knew she could not live long." His voice died into silence, and, daring to steal a glance at him, April saw that his face was a mask from which all feeling had fled. His voice was flat as he continued. " When she died I took Constancia, for her father was so overcome that he seemed scarcely to know what to do with her. A year later he too died—he was killed in a motor accident while travelling abroad—and Constancia became my legal ward. She has grown up in my care, and she will of course enjoy my protection until the time that she marries."

"What a—what a tragic story!" April said, or heard herself saying.

He nodded, but there was still no warmth or feeling in his voice as he echoed her:

"A very tragic story!"

"I understand now why you feel that you have to spoil her."

Instantly his face lightened, and his handsome mouth curved at the corners with humour.

"I do not so much spoil her as give way to her for the sake of peace. She is a somewhat turbulent personality, as you yourself must have recognized at once when you saw her for the first time yesterday. But in addition to the turbulence—the wildness, on occasion—there is a quality of sweetness which is difficult to resist sometimes. Sweetness and truth and honesty, and—I'll confess!—determination. And when these are allied to the charm of a woman's face, albeit she is a girl in years..."

"You can't resist her."

"Perhaps not," he admitted once more. "Perhaps that is the real reason why she twists me so easily around her finger!"

As she dwelt upon this April felt her amazement gradually grow. And she had thought him hard... a type it would be almost impossible to impress! Yet a sixteen-year-old girl had the art of twisting him round her finger!

"Has she ever been away to school?" April asked.

"No, she was taught at home, and my sister has taken her on various holidays. As I think we mentioned, she has been to England."

"And Doña Ignatia is as devoted to her as you are?"

"I would say that is the case, yes."

"She is a fortunate girl," April remarked, but what she was actually thinking was that Doña Ignatia, with her wise eyes, probably realized, as he did not, that the young girl's passionate devotion to her guardian had lately turned into a passionate adoration that was in no sense of the word an adoration of the mind. Like most Spanish girls she had developed rapidly, and, midway between sixteen and seventeen, she had fallen in love in a possessive, physical sense.

As she walked at Don Carlos's side in the brilliant

morning sunshine April was aware of a sudden uneasiness that had started to grow at the back of her own mind. And it wasn't in connection with the lovely Constancia only. Now that she had heard something about Constancia's mother she felt she had been supplied with a key to the whole personality of Don Carlos de Formera y Santos.

At eighteen he had fallen in love, and his love disappointed him. In addition to that she died while he was still wholeheartedly devoted to her, and the chances that he would ever forget her now were possibly very remote. By making her daughter a part of his life he had made her an imperishable part, too, and any woman who fell in love with him would find it difficult to dislodge the pair of them. Difficult to establish for herself a place in his heart, even if she succeeded in making for herself a place in his life.

The morning sunshine fell less goldenly for April, and she wanted to protest suddenly and unreasonably. She wanted to delve suddenly and deeply into the question of his affections, and reassure herself on one point, at least. That he was not at the moment in love with anyone.

Because she could not possibly do this she asked:

"And are there any other members of your family that I have yet to meet?"

"Several," he answered, smiling carelessly. "One or two uncles and an aunt, a few cousins. And," as a small pale blue car travelled under the arch towards them, "my half-brother, Rodrigo. He is here to breakfast with us, or so it would seem. He looks after my vineyards and has a small house of his own a couple of smiles or so from here."

The pale blue car braked, and then stopped, and by

the time they reached it Rodrigo de Formera was standing beside it and watching their approach with a slight smile of incredulity on his devastatingly handsome face.

He was a typical young Spaniard of the upper classes, but he had far more than a typical Spaniard's good looks. Even his brother's paled into insignificance beside them, although the quality of Don Carlos's appeal for the opposite sex did not depend merely on his looks. It was in everything about him, and particularly in his arrogance, and air of complete assurance. Rodrigo, on the other hand, had an almost feminine appeal, made up of big brown slightly sloping eyes that were not many shades darker than April's own, perfectly chiselled features and thick black curly hair that glistened like oiled silk in the sunshine.

He advanced to meet them when a bare foot or so separated them and greeted his brother with a little salute.

"You are up early, *amigo*! You returned last night, and this morning you could not wait to be in the saddle, is that it?" He bowed with excessive formality to April, the surprise in his eyes so unconcealed that it brought a little smile to her lips. Although when his admiration got the better of his surprise, and she was treated to the full blaze of it, she felt the colour rise up in her cheeks and spread wildly. "Good morning, *señorita*! This is indeed an honour!"

Don Carlos looked for an instant amused, and then his amusement vanished. He made the introduction curtly.

"My brother, Rodrigo, April. Rodrigo, my wife-to-be . . . Miss April Day!"

Rodrigo's astonishment was almost ludicrous.

"Wife-to-be?" It was quite plain he had not seen Doña Ignatia for several days. "But this is delightful news, although so unexpected that I find it hard to take in! You must forgive me, Miss Day, if I appear as if I am completely astounded, and, as a matter of fact, I am..." He looked helplessly at Carlos, his dark brows knitted, and then a somewhat perplexed expression crossed his face. "And you are English! We were fairly certain Carlos would take an English wife one day, but..."

Carlos intervened.

"You have declared yourself astounded, and we are prepared to believe you, Rodrigo. Now, since you are here, you will come in to breakfast. That was, no doubt, your intention?"

"Of course." But Rodrigo was finding it difficult to recover from his surprise. "I had no idea you were back until I passed José on the road just now. You look as if your stay in Madrid agreed with you. But of course," making a little gesture with his hands, while his eyes laughed, "if you found there a wife... and, if I may say so, such a very beautiful one! I shall be happy to have you for a sister-in-law, *señorita*!"

During breakfast he talked a great deal, making frequent gestures with his hands, always including April in the conversation. His eyes found it difficult to leave her face, and although his admiration was a little overwhelming it began gradually to amuse her again when she realized it was purely spontaneous. Neither Doña Ignatia nor Constancia made their appearance in the cool, bare room where breakfast was served, and April made up her mind that in future she too would breakfast in her own quarters—after all, she had been provided with a sitting-room of her own. And it was probably considered the thing to do if one happened to be a woman.

But as she poured out coffee for the other two, and helped herself to fruit juice and a delicious ripe peach, she was glad of the preoccupation while Rodrigo's slightly bemused brown eyes rested on her. He seemed to be completely fascinated by her softly falling brown hair, and the delicacy of her skin, and all the time that unmistakable perplexity remained at the back of his eyes, and every time he looked at his brother he seemed to be trying to read his mind. To get at the bottom of a riddle.

"You ride, *señorita*?" he asked eagerly, when the coffee-pot was empty, and all three were smoking cigarettes. "You rode with Carlos this morning?"

She shook her head.

"No, that was Constancia."

"Ah, Constancia!" He glanced at her curiously, as if he was wondering what she thought of her future husband's ward, and whether her coming had been entirely appreciated by Constancia. "She rides well alone, but she prefers to ride pillion with Carlos."

"I've never seen anyone ride pillion on the back of a horse until this morning."

"Then you must become accustomed to seeing it in Andalusia. You must try it yourself, *señorita*." He leaned towards her, his eyes suddenly audacious. "If not with Carlos, then with myself. I am a better horse-man than Carlos."

"But when April rides pillion it will be with me," Carlos told him with much and quite unmistakable crispness.

Rodrigo sighed, and ran slim brown fingers through his silky black curls.

"Ah, yes, of course... you two are betrothed! I had forgotten!" His eyes glinted mockingly as they turned once more to his brother. "It is difficult to believe so much has been settled in so short a time, when the last time I saw you you were a free man, Carlos!"

"Important decisions do not take a great deal of time to arrive at," Carlos returned, with a displeased expression in his black eyes. Then he rose purposefully from the table. "I have much to discuss with you, Rodrigo. I shall require a full report from you of all that has happened in my absence, and now is an excellent time to hear some of your news. If you will pardon us, April," inclining his head towards her politely. "I have no doubt you can find some means of entertaining yourself this morning. Late this afternoon, when it is cooler, I will take you for a drive and let you see something of the countryside which I'm afraid you missed last night."

Rodrigo held out his hand at parting.

"April," he said softly. "It is a charming name! Am I, as a prospective brother-in-law, permitted to call you April?"

"Of course," April answered.

Don Carlos did not look too pleased.

"So long as you do not make comments every time you use it I suppose I cannot reasonably object," he said.

CHAPTER VIII

BUT the late afternoon drive half promised by Carlos did not, after all, become a reality. Some people arrived just before tea, and April was summoned from her room to meet them.

She had retired after lunch for a siesta, following the example of Doña Ignatia and Constancia, although she would have much preferred to sit in the cool of one of the verandas with a book. But that was not considered correct in this very Spanish household, and she had to resign herself to at least a couple of hours in the absolute hush of her room, with the shutters closed and a green twilight making the hug carved bed seem a trifle grotesque, and the vast wardrobe and dressing-table seem even more grotesque.

She lay staring into the dimness for about an hour, and then got up and sat beside her shutters for another hour, peering between the slats at the golden world outside. And it was while she was doing this that she saw the slim cream car glide round an angle of the house and slip beneath the arch into the courtyard.

It was still very warm, and she changed into something very cool, and the colour of a pale pink carnation. She slipped her feet into open-toed white sandals, added a touch of cologne, to her temples and the backs of her hands, picked up a white purse handbag containing a fresh handkerchief and the usual mirror in which to peep at herself when necessary, and sat waiting for the moment when she felt she might emerge from her room without transgressing any rules.

But barely had she sat herself down to wait than there came a knock on her door, and the maid who had been deputed to wait on her came to tell her that Doña Ignatia was entertaining visitors in the main *sala*, and would like her to join her as soon as possible.

April stood up, feeling relieved, but she wondered who the visitors were, and whether they had any connection with the white car she had seen slipping under the arch. When she got down to the *sala* she no longer had to wonder, for the two ladies were both wearing brilliant yellow, and it was a flash of canary yellow that had attracted her eye when the car first appeared round the corner of the house.

Doña Ignatia mentioned the name of the elder lady first.

"Lady Hartingdon, wife of Sir James Hartingdon, who was British Ambassador to Madrid for several years. Lady Hartingdon was so devoted to this country that she persuaded her husband to settle in it."

"As a matter of fact it was the other way round," Lady Hartingdon asserted. For an exceptionally plump English matron she was not entirely suited to yellow shantung with large white blobs on it, and a vast picture hat lined with yellow, but although she had a slightly peevish face her small blue eyes were bright with interest as they roved over April. "And there was the servant problem at home, and all that sort of thing. I couldn't see how we were going to manage, so I agreed it would be a good thing to stay out here." She offered a limp hand to April. "I understand you're going to marry Don Carlos, my dear. You've certainly given us all a surprise!"

The other, much younger woman—not a bit like her, so it was difficult to think of them as mother and daughter—wearing a green skirt and a yellow sun-top, also offered her hand. She had jade-green eyes that were quite remarkable, a chrysanthemum mop of bronzish-red curls, and a figure that was tall and graceful enough to be the figure of a model.

"Nice to meet you," she said, as she, too, studied April with quite unconcealed interest. "I couldn't believe it when word got round that Carlos had got himself engaged to marry a girl from the Old Country! And you are English, aren't you...? Yes, of course you are, with a complexion like that, and a name that couldn't be anything other than English! But when Carlos went to Madrid about a month ago we had no idea he was planning matrimony!"

"As a matter of fact, I—I don't think he was," April returned awkwardly, not knowing quite what to say while the other was staring at her so hard, and so suspiciously. For, although her voice was friendly, and even her eyes had an alert, friendly smile in them, at the back of those eyes April sensed there was something that was not at all friendly. And the brevity of her handshake had indicated a disinclination to go through with such a formality at all.

"You mean you've only recently met, and it's one of those whirlwind affairs? Love at first sight, and that sort of thing? Marriage the natural outcome!"

"I—well, I don't know about that..."

"Jessica, my dear, don't put so many impertinent questions," Lady Hartingdon intervened, fanning herself with one of her gloves, although the room was beautifully cool. "You can't expect Miss Day to enjoy being catechized by you, and it really isn't any affair of yours."

She was sitting on the edge of one of the tapestry-covered chairs, and Doña Ignatia was pouring out tea with a certain awkwardness at a handsome tea-equipage which had just been wheeled into the room. There were little cakes and biscuits, and the tea was pale and straw-coloured, and became even more straw-coloured when cream was added. The ladies all, with the exception of April, refused sugar, and Lady Hartingdon asked for lemon because her figure was getting out of hand. It occurred to April that the operative word should have been "got," and not "getting."

Don Carlos was not in the room, and neither was Constancia. Doña Ignatia explained that her brother was having a busy day inspecting the estate, and going into details connected with it, but she offered no apology for Constancia's absence.

Jessica Hartingdon disposed of several little cakes, and all the time her eyes were on April. April felt certain that there was no detail of her dress, her looks —everything about her—that escaped the other girl, and she began to feel so acutely uncomfortable at last that Lady Hartingdon once more came to her rescue. Although it was doubtful whether that was what she intended.

"I must say we never thought to have an English neighbour here at the Casa Formera, although when you marry Don Carlos you'll become Spanish, won't you? I wonder how you'll like that?" She nibbled a biscuit, and fanned herself vigorously with the glove in her free hand. "Yes; I wonder how you'll like that, my dear? I always say it's one thing to live in a country, but quite another to live as the natives do, if you'll forgive me, my dear Doña Ignatia, for referring to all you delightful people as 'natives'!"

Doña Ignatia retained an expression of calm inscrutability, and Jessica rested her head against the carved back of the chair behind her and inquired with a sidelong look at April:

"How did Constancia take the news when it was broken to her? Or are you only in a position to guess?"

April's expression grew more alert, and she measured the curiously veiled glance of the late Ambassador's daughter with rather a level one of her own.

"Is there any reason why she should not have accepted it as normal? After all, she must always have expected her guardian to marry one day."

"One day... yes!" The green eyes glistened curiously, and Jessica leaned forward to make a confidential aside. "But that isn't precisely the point. With Constancia it isn't the day that is of so much importance, but her guardian's choice of a bride. And I don't suppose you've known her long enough to have the least idea what sort of a bride she'd foist upon Don Carlos!"

Her mother murmured something warningly, and Jessica took the hint. She smiled complacently and said:

"We're having a cocktail party on the fourteenth. You must persuade Don Carlos to bring you."

But Don Carlos himself suddenly made his appearance in the *sala*, and she jumped up and greeted him with so much enthusiasm that April was not surprised Doña Ignatia tightened her lips and looked prim.

But Jessica Hartingdon plainly looked upon the Spaniard as an old and close friend, and she made no attempt to conceal the pleasure that leapt into her eyes when she first realized he was standing there in the opening of the tall french windows. He was wearing one of his light, beautifully-cut suits, and as always he looked immaculate, with a tie that flowed carelessly although it was meticulously knotted, and impeccable linen. He might, for him, have been having a hectic afternoon connected with his own interests, but his appearance was cool and calm and collected, as if he was newly bathed, newly shaved, and smelling slightly of shaving cream and after-shave lotion.

He came into the middle of the room and smiled when he caught sight of the visitors. Before permitting Jessica to annex him and pour forth her congratulations he bowed in front of her mother and inquired after her health, inquired after the health and well-being of Sir James Hartingdon, and then turned to the redhead, who had flushed engagingly at the very moment that she realized his presence, and met the full blaze of delight in the jade-green eyes.

But Jessica was also reproachful. She laid a hand on his sleeve, and shook her head at him.

"You didn't even tell us you were going away to Madrid! And now that you are back we hear that you're engaged to be married!"

He smiled charmingly, with a quirk of humour at the corner of his mouth.

"News travels fast. You heard this from my sister, of course? She has already made you and my fiancée known to one another?"

"Of course I have been introduced to Miss Day," she returned, a little impatiently. "But it wasn't from

Doña Ignatia that I heard of your engagement... at least, not in the first place. As you say, news—good news!—travels fast, and I should think everyone in the district was aware of the surprise you had prepared for us in Madrid by this time yesterday afternoon. That, I believe, was the time you were expected back?"

"And you knew of that too?" His voice was smooth, but his expression was dry.

Jessica's colour increased, and her mother said hurriedly:

"We simply couldn't wait to congratulate you, Don Carlos, and although I never allow anything to interfere with my afternoon siestas normally I said to Jessica that whatever else she had on hand, she simply *must* bring me over here to let you know how happy we are you are to be married at last!"

"That was most kind," he said, and bowed gravely. "Most kind!"

If anything, Jessica's colour heightened. But her green eyes flashed a few unexpected sparks.

"Yes, it was, wasn't it, Carlos?" she murmured, looking directly at him. "So little time lost, and all because we were so keen to meet your fiancée!"

"And, now that you have met her," he said suavely, moving over until he stood behind April's chair, and placing a hand lightly on her shoulder, "I hope you feel that you two will get along well together? After all, you are both English, and that should be a bond."

"Oh, it is a bond, certainly," Jessica agreed casually, pulling on her gloves. "But I may not be here very much longer. I'm hoping to get a job modelling, in

97

either London or Paris. I have actually been offered something."

"That doesn't surprise me in the least," Carlos returned, with the same suavity. "With your so delightful appearance I'm sure you will prove quite a sensation."

For a long moment she looked at him, as if she was endeavouring to convince herself that he was absolutely serious, and not mocking her in a strange, polite way. And then she said almost defensively:

"But, of course, I want to be here for your wedding. I wouldn't miss that for anything!"

"And we wouldn't have you miss it for anything," he replied.

She bit her full lower lip hard, with some very white and perfect teeth.

"Have you any plans yet?" she asked, somewhat jerkily. "Is the wedding to be soon?"

"We have only been betrothed for a fortnight... a little less than that," Don Carlos told her, his black eyes unflinching as he gazed at her, and also a little humorous. "You would not rush us into marriage before we have had an opportunity to become accustomed to the idea of being betrothed, would you?"

Jessica's eyes gleamed again.

"But you must have known one another some little while..."

"Barely three weeks altogether," he surprised April considerably by admitting softly. "But it is astonishshing how little time one needs when one's mind is made up!"

"Obviously," Jessica murmured, plainly surprised. Then her eyes narrowed. "But there is such a thing as marrying in haste and repenting at leisure!"

98

Don Carlos's affable expression did not waver.

"That is what I mean to avoid," he said. "Wasn't it Jacob who waited seven years for his Rachel? I do not intend to wait seven years for April, but seven weeks, seven months... who knows?"

April had an extraordinary sensation as she sat there, his hand upon her shoulder, his breath lightly stirring her hair, while he and Jessica went on exchanging utterly uninformative looks, and their conversation sounded as if they were engaged in a kind of wordy duel. Soft-spoken sentences that were like lightning flashes, each seeking to find a mark or parry a thrust.

And seven weeks, seven months... what did he mean by that? When she had no feeling at all that they would ever be married!

"And of course, there is Constancia you have to consider, haven't you?" Jessica put in smoothly, as if she realized she was delivering a kind of final thrust. "She has always been a bit of a problem, hasn't she? And now you may find she is a very big problem!"

Lady Hartingdon rose hurriedly.

"Darling, I think we ought to go now," she said.

They departed after a series of bows and smiles and handshakes, with Don Carlos escorting them out to their car.

"And you *will* bring your fiancée to our cocktail party on the fourteenth, won't you?" Jessica purred smoothly as she drove away.

That night, after dinner, April wandered for a while in the garden, while Don Carlos attended to some pressing business in his library, and Doña Ignatia sat

99

beneath a soft flood of lamplight in the *sala* and put infinitely tiny stitches into her sewing.

The night was warm ... not with the dried up, suffocating warmth of Madrid, but a velvety warmth that was tempered by the breezes from the sea. How many flower-scents floated in the atmosphere around her April could only guess, and how many stars burned brilliantly in the clear sky above her she could not even begin to guess. She only knew that they were like lamps hanging near the earth, and the golden crescent of the young moon had increased to a pale slice of melon shedding a faint light across the garden.

Wearing something cool and diaphanous, April drifted like a wraith, not consciously thinking of anything, not even attempting to dwell upon the future. And then Don Carlos came striding briskly over the paths to look for her, and she practically collided with him as she turned to walk back to the house.

Instantly his arms closed round her, to prevent her from stumbling, and she made a clutching movement at the front of his dinner jacket. She didn't really realize what she was doing until she felt his eyes peering down at her through the gloom, and looking upwards quickly she met the faint sparkle of humour in the night-dark depths, and saw in the light of the moon that his lips were curving quizzically.

"I might have hurt you," he said, "coming so quickly along the path." His voice grew soft, anxious. "I didn't hurt you, did I, *cara*? You are so small it would be easy to trample you underfoot!"

She tried to laugh, but her laugh sounded self-conscious.

"I'm not as small as all that. And I'm afraid I was hurrying too."

"Because you were afraid?" There was a quality in his voice that disturbed her, shook her. He was still, in spite of the fact that she had released his dinner jacket, holding her lightly in his arms, and her head with its swinging dark hair was on a level with his white dress tie. She could smell the fragrance of his tobacco as his breath set the shining hair stirring softly, and if she'd moved her head but a fraction she would have touched the square tip of his dark chin. "You are not afraid of the garden at night, are you, *amada*? There is nothing in it to hurt you! Although I would prefer that you didn't wander in it alone!"

She felt as if all her pulses were leaping and bounding riotously.

"You don't imagine I expect an escort every time I go for a walk at night, do you?" she said, a little incoherently. "In England I often go for walks by myself, at night and any other time that I feel like it."

He replied somewhat soberly, allowing his arms to drop, but slipping a hand beneath her elbow as he guided her back along the paths:

"I have a feeling that in England you do many things I would not approve ... many things our girls would not be allowed to do!"

"Such as?" she couldn't resist inquiring, turning her face towards him, and her eyes up to him.

He looked down at her with eyes that were very dark indeed.

"You have affairs with young men that would be frowned upon here. You go to cinemas with them, and to dances. You have a strange freedom with young men of your own age ... a dangerous freedom!"

She smiled for an instant, and then assured him:

"I know very few young men of my own age ... and I hardly ever go to dances. To the cinema sometimes, of course."

"Escorted by a young man?"

She smiled again.

"There was one young man once ... but only for a very short time."

"And how old were you?"

"Eighteen."

He frowned swiftly.

"And did you imagine yourself—in love with this young man?"

"Oh, no." There was no doubt about the decisiveness of that. "I have never been in love. I don't suppose I ever will be ... now," she added, in so low a voice that he could hardly hear it. But she realized that he had heard it when he stopped and regarded her gravely, putting his fingers under her chin and lifting it to peer once more into her eyes.

"And why not now?" he asked, very quietly.

She found it impossible to answer.

"Because you have consented to marry me? Because in future there will be no other man in your life but—me!"

It was certainly a shattering reminder, but it shattered her in quite another way as well. It made her feel suddenly weak at the knees, a little breathless, as if she had been running, over-quick to lower her eyes as she felt his eyes piercing the velvety shadows of the night and boring their way into hers.

"Love comes to all of us, sooner or later," he told

her quietly. "We none of us know quite when it is coming, but it does come. Sometimes it grows out of affection, sometimes it is the result of a single meeting, sometimes it is the cause of a lot of bitter unhappiness. Perhaps the most worthwhile love is the love that grows out of affection..." speaking in such a brooding voice that she was almost mesmerized by it. "But the love that one remembers is the love that hurts!"

He released her chin abruptly, and she knew he was thinking of Constancia's mother. Her heart sank... she couldn't prevent it sinking; and she couldn't prevent herself feeling that the night was no more beautiful and filled with magic than any other night she had known.

The love that grows out of affection... Was that the love he felt for Constancia?

Why, oh, why had he asked her to marry him? What had he meant when he told her that, by agreeing to marry him, she would be solving a problem for him? He had taken words out of her mouth... *"You happened to me at just the right moment!"*

But, for her, it had been the wrong moment! She felt it; she knew it. If she ever did marry him she would be paving the way to bitter unhappiness for herself. Her whole future would lie in ruins, and all because she had allowed him to over-persuade her... because his will was stronger than hers, and he could, apparently, force her to his will! He could force her to become his wife, give her nothing but security, and that was why her future would lie in ruins...

For security was not what she wanted... not security and nothing else! She knew that in a blinding flash of knowledge that affected her with dizziness, as if the stars had lurched in concert in the great void above her head, and the path that was a checkerboard of light and shadow had lurched, too, like the deck of a heaving ship.

She wanted much, much more than security, but she was too staggered to put a name to what she actually did want. She only knew that if she didn't get it...

"The love one remembers is the love that hurts!..."

Oh, no! she thought, shying away from the word like a frightened colt shying from something that had startled it. Don't let me fall in love!... Not with Don Carlos, who has loved once, and is possibly on the verge of loving again! Only he doesn't really know about this second love. He merely suspects it, and is protecting himself against it... by announcing his intention of marrying me!

She felt his hand grasping her arm again.

"We will go back to the house."

CHAPTER IX

DURING the next week Don Carlos took April for several drives in the surrounding countryside.

She discovered that it was mostly flat, and in places it reminded her of open desert, it was so scorched and bare, apart from the esparto grass and thorny plants that loved the dry, arid atmosphere. As far as the eye could see vast stretches of it quivered in the heat that had been known to cause mirages, and southwards there was always the sea, the deep blue Mediterranean that ran like an azure ribbon between it and the untroubled horizon.

But Andalusia is a flowery land, a centre of sugar-cane plantations and vineyards, as well as open spaces. Towns like Cadiz and Cordova, famed for other things apart from beauty, are, in themselves, bowers of flowers, and are set amidst orchards of lucious fruit; and in Santa Cruz the streets are so narrow that clematis and jasmine form arches across them and smother the balconies of houses opposite. Jerez produces sherry, and its vineyards lie close to it, extending along the flat coastal belt to San Lucar, which is about fifty miles south of Seville.

April saw Seville for the second time when Don Carlos took her to view the cathedral, which is the pride and the pomp and the circumstance of Seville. Its nave is so vast that the beholder feels dwarfed by it, and the door of the Pardon recalls the days when Andalusia was under the influence of the Moors. He also took her to see the Giralda, which is so reminiscent of the Moorish period that it might almost be a minaret set down on the African side of the Mediterranean, instead of in modern Seville. The lovely pale pink shape of it, etched against the hard blue of the sky, had April quite entranced.

Afterwards they had lunch at a very up-to-date hotel where the food was deliciously Spanish, and then they sat for a while in the cool of some gardens and drove home past the prickly pear and the cactus to find the white house with its pantiled roofs shaking off its afternoon inertia, and Rodrigo being entertained by Constancia in the big *patio* at the back of the house.

Constancia was wearing slacks—a daring thing to do in a house presided over by Doña Ignatia, who as yet knew nothing about them—and she was parading them in front of Rodrigo with an air of being very well convinced that they became her, although she was also a little afraid of her own daring.

"Señorita Day wears slacks," she said, in extenuation. "Not often, but I have seen her wearing them in the early mornings, when she thinks no one is about who can take exception. I watch her often from my window when she is walking in the garden."

"Señorita Day is English," Rodrigo pointed out, "and the English do many things Spanish girls are not permitted to do." His voice was light and teasing. "And why do you watch her in secret? Are you envious of her golden looks, that have twined themselves about the heart of my dear brother Carlos?"

An extraordinary expression stole into Constancia's eyes. It was almost a calculating expression, and she caught her scarlet lower lip up between her teeth and bit it hard for a moment.

"She is charming, isn't she?" she said slowly. "Very English ... very lovely in a quiet, unexciting way. But not as lovely as Señorita Hartingdon, who has red hair, and eyes of a quite unusual colour. I have heard it said that my guardian was very attracted by Sir James Hartingdon's daughter!"

"But not enough to marry her," Rodrigo observed, rolling a long, thin Spanish cigarette between his fingers. "It is Miss Day he has asked to marry him, and being a man I am not surprised. She is fragile as blown glass, and her eyes, too, are unusual ... looking into them I have the feeling I am looking into twin lakes of limpid gold," sending a cloud of fragrant smoke into the still air, and speaking almost dreamily.

Constancia glanced at him contemptuously.

"And does a man wish a creature as fragile as glass for a wife? She is stupid, and she cannot even ride! ... She is afraid of Fadia, the beautiful new chestnut! Señorita Hartingdon—although I have no love for her personally!" with emphasis—"rides well."

"A small matter," Rodrigo dismissed the comparison with that lazy, mocking sparkle in his eyes, that were so fantastically handsome. "It is not in the least essential that a wife should ride, and the finer the glass the more resistant it often is. That goes for many things, my child," wagging a finger at her as if he was attempting to teach her a lesson. "You must not be so easily deceived, and it is not a good thing to make comparisons. In any case," regarding her between his thick eyelashes, "you are not trying to tell me that you would prefer it if Señorita Hartingdon became the wife of Don Carlos?"

He was so certain that she loathed the very thought

of any woman—even one of her own countrywomen—becoming the wife of Don Carlos that he was not in the least surprised when she rose to the bait or the soft taunt in his voice.

"Of course I would not prefer it! I do not wish him to marry anyone... *anyone*! At least——" Her slim breasts heaved, her eyes flashed stormily, she bit her lip again revealingly... until a thin trickle of blood ran down her chin. "One day I would wish him to marry someone..."

"You, perhaps?" Rodrigo said softly. "In about another year, when you are less of a hoyden, and more of a woman."

"I am not a hoyden," she said distinctly, her eyes seeking to transfix him, as a blaze of lightning might do. "And I am a woman already!"

"But not in those slacks," he taunted.

"Señorita Day wears them," she reminded him. "And she is a woman."

He agreed with a certain amount of fervour.

"She is, indeed. The sort of woman a man might dream of... I wonder how, and by what means, Carlos got in touch with her? How he got to know her! There is a certain amount of mystery about this sudden betrothal."

"That is what Doña Ignatia says," Constancia told him, almost eagerly. "It is not an ordinary betrothal. They do not know one another very well... they do not talk easily together. She is a little afraid of him, and he is more formal with her than he is with Señorita Hartingdon. He does not look at her as a man looks at a woman he loves and desires!"

Rodrigo smiled slightly.

"And what do you know of love and desire, little

one? Does Carlos look at you sometimes as if he might desire you one day?"

She seemed to withdraw into a shell.

"He loved my mother," she said sullenly.

"But that does not mean it naturally follows that he will one day love you! You are foolish to count upon it... if you *are* counting upon it?"

She smiled in a Mona Lisa fashion.

"I do not believe this marriage will come to anything. Doña Ignatia does not believe it will come to anything."

"Indeed?" Rodrigo said. He regarded her thoughtfully, then he looked suddenly disgusted. "Women," he remarked, "are only happy when they are scheming for the downfall of someone they dislike, but I would not count upon it that my brother Carlos is not secretly burning with love for little English April. I could very easily burn with love for her myself," he concluded, and Constancia's eyes blazed with an entirely different set of sparks.

"You!" she exclaimed. "She is not for you, in any case! And Don Carlos has it planned that you will marry Juanita Ribieros. She is very pretty, her parents are rich, and she will make you a very good wife."

His eyebrows arched mockingly.

"I believe it has also crossed his mind that *you* might make me a good wife... It would be one way of disposing of you! Your parents were not rich, but they left you a small amount of property, and together we might manage..."

But it was at that moment that Don Carlos's car slid under the arch, and he was spared the indignation of Constancia because her guardian might wish to dispose of her in some way or other, at some time in the immediate or distant future. Her cheeks were red with anger, however, and her eyes fairly blazing with resentment when he opened the car door for April, and the two of them crossed the *patio*.

"What in the world are you doing dressed like that?" Don Carlos demanded, his expression as cold as ice as he reviewed the pale violet slacks.

Constancia shrank, her anger evaporating before the concentrated fury in her guardian's eyes.

"I... I bought them many weeks ago, when I was in Cadiz," she explained falteringly. "I was with Señorita Hartingdon at the time... She persuaded me. She said all girls wear them in her country."

"That may be so," Don Carlos returned blisteringly, "but what young girls wear in Señorita Hartingdon's country is no concern of yours. It is no concern of mine, and you are my ward."

"But Señorita Day... April," she managed, since he had more or less ordered her to drop the absurd formality she was continually striving to restore between herself and April only a couple of days ago, "April wears them. In the mornings I have seen her!"

'That, too, is nothing to do with you."

"But if it is not respectable to wear slacks——"

"In Spain we do not consider it respectable. You will go to your room and change out of them, and afterwards you may destroy them. Now go!"

April intervened.

"Oh, but really——!"

"I said go!" Don Carlos's voice was quite relentless.

Doña Ignatia appeared at the head of the veranda steps. She was wearing a dress of rich purple silk, in

110

spite of the heat of the day, and her pale face was smooth and bland.

"What is it, Carlos?" she asked, the cooing of doves and pigeons in the softness and meekness of her voice.

"I have ordered Constancia to go to her room and get rid of her offensive dress," he replied brusquely. "It is an offence to the eye."

His sister spread her hands, and shrugged her shoulders.

"Of course I agree with you, but Miss Day appears in similar costume in the mornings. It is not entirely fair——"

"It doesn't matter what Miss Day does!"

"I see," Doña Ignatia said, as if she saw a great deal more than was actually intended, her eyes widening in her paper-white face. "Then, in that case, Constancia, go to your room!"

April felt the hot blood mantling her cheeks. Her usually very gentle eyes glittered.

"I'm sorry if I've been guilty of a rather bad *faux pas,*" she exclaimed. "But I'd no idea I was seen wearing slacks. They're comfortable, and I was careful to keep out of the way of the windows. But if it's not respectable for Constancia to wear them——"

"Constancia is my ward," he snapped coldly. "Her behaviour is important."

"And mine is not?"

His eyes were as remote as northern ice fields, and although he glanced at her for an instant in faint surprise there was no apology in his voice—only added impatience—as he continued:

"She is being groomed for an important role in life. It is essential that no false ideas should be put into her

111

head, or anything that will interfere with the full flowering of my plans for her permitted for a single instant." The concentrated fury in his voice was a revelation to her, the sharpness of his tone enough to make any young woman who was engaged to him feel amazed. Especially when he spoke to her like that in front of his closest relatives. "If you must be informal, please don't try and communicate your notions to Constancia. Please avoid trying to influence her, as Miss Hartingdon has so obviously striven to influence her!"

April was astounded, but she was not quite abashed. She turned away, biting her lip, her golden eyes agleam with humiliation and anger at the same time, and Rodrigo came to her quickly and whispered:

"Don't take any notice! When Carlos is angry he seldom spares anyone, but it is simply that he is angry..."

"Thank you," she replied, without attempting to modulate her voice. "But so far as I'm aware, I have done nothing to arouse his anger! Perhaps I too had better go to my room."

But Rodrigo detained her with a hand on her arm.

"Please!—I am here for just a short while!" His shatteringly handsome eyes were full of undisguised pleading. "Do not go, *señorita,* when there is no need..."

Doña Ignatia had repeated her command to Constancia to leave them, and the girl had fled silently up the steps and become swallowed up by the silent dimness of the house. Don Carlos turned to his brother and demanded to know what he was doing there.

112

"You are leaving for Madrid in the morning. Have you not plans... last-minute arrangements to make?"

"My arrangements are all made, *amigo,*" Rodrigo replied soothingly. "But my man, Jaime, has been called away to the sick-bed of his father, and his wife is a poor cook, so I thought perhaps I could stay here to dinner. Even, perhaps, occupy my old room for the night?"

"You can, of course," Don Carlos assured him coldly. "Your room is yours whenever you wish to occupy it, but in future try to give us some warning when a visit from you is imminent."

Rodrigo looked quietly jubilant.

"I will," he promised. "But Constancia saw to it that I was entertained. That young woman is quite capable of receiving visitors when Ignatia is resting, or is not free to do so."

"I have no doubt," his half-brother snapped. "But you are not an ordinary visitor, and you have a habit of upsetting her, which I do not approve. Apart from my annoyance just now because she was unsuitably clad, I was annoyed because you had so obviously been baiting her, and she was agitated. In future you will not amuse yourself at her expense, do you understand, *señor?*"

At the excessive formality Rodrigo's eyebrows rose, and then he grinned impudently, and just a trifle wickedly, across at April.

"I understand, *amigo!*"

"Then go to your room and unpack whatever you have brought with you for the night."

As Rodrigo disappeared—following another jubilant smile directed quite deliberately at April—Don

113

Carlos took April by the arm and purposefully led her away along the path instead of permitting her to enter the house also, as she had been on the point of doing. She felt shiny-nosed and dusty, after the heat and the long day devoted principally to sight-seeing, and she was longing for a bath in her opulent bathroom, and a complete change of garments. But Don Carlos thought otherwise, at any rate for the moment.

"I want to talk to you for a few minutes," he said, leading her away from the house and along an ilex-bordered path to a remote corner of the garden, where on a sort of raised terrace that looked out towards the distant sea, some garden chairs were arranged in the shelter of a kind of natural arbour. "If you will be so good as to listen to me!"

April said absolutely nothing, feeling perhaps angrier than she had ever felt in her life before. She had been made to look trifling, and a little vulgar—to say the least!—in front of Doña Ignatia and Rodrigo, to say nothing of a black-eyed, sixteen-year-old girl who hated her. Of that she was quite convinced. And it was one reason why her anger had got out of hand, for although Don Carlos had rebuked Constancia, he had also championed her. He had admitted that his anger was partly due to the fact that Constancia looked agitated.

And that meant that Constancia must mean a very great deal to him... A very great deal!

Which was natural, perhaps, but not so natural that it explained the reason why he dismissed April as unimportant. At least, not when she was officially engaged to marry him!

"You will sit here," he said, and pulled out a chair for her. His dark eyes regarded her for a moment with

114

a flickering of interest. She was trying to get the better of her secret agitation by clenching her hands rather tightly as they were held down at her sides, and she was biting her lip hard, because for some absurd reason her lower one didn't feel very steady. Her eyes had a somewhat fixed expression in them.

The sun, that was shedding a warm path across the sea, fell goldenly all about them, and the air was full of sweet scents, and the coolness that the approach of evening nearly always brought. Although sometimes, after dark, the heat seemed to return again, and the nights were very breathless.

"I should not," Don Carlos remarked, still observing her, "have said what I said in front of you just now. You will forgive me?"

She shrugged.

"There is nothing to forgive. You were angry, and you wanted to make your ward understand that her dress was outrageous."

He frowned.

"But that could have been done without involving you. I apologize!"

She spread her hands ... a gesture she had probably copied from him, and Rodrigo, who was much more Latin.

"It doesn't matter. But I'm sorry I gave Constancia the opportunity to copy me. I should have been more discreet in such a household as yours."

His black brows actually met as he frowned this time, but there was the merest suspicion of a twinkle at the very backs of his eyes.

"But you were discreet. You chose the early mornings for your appearance in the type of semi-masculine garb we frown upon here, and although it is true I

115

have glimpsed you myself..." He paused, the twinkle becoming more noticeable. "And I must say you looked very delightful! A charming boy! But it is not a boy a man wishes to marry!"

"Of course not," primly.

"It is a woman who can look really feminine in the clothes that were designed for her... softly falling skirts and draperies that make the most of her naturally graceful shape, and not harsh outlines that conceal them. A woman in trousers is an offence in Spanish eyes, because she is not a true woman. But that does not mean she may not be permitted to wear them occasionally, if they please her... and she happens to be English!"

April had not been able to resist a smile at his picture of an ultra-feminine woman in ultra-feminine draperies, but her lips tautened again when she caught the condescension in his voice. She was not making any apologies for being English!

"But it was Señorita Hartingdon who persuaded Constancia to forgo her feminine appeal at odd moments," Don Carlos continued. "On a shopping expedition together, apparently. So no real blame attaches to you for the metamorphosis I saw this afternoon... Constancia as I do not wish to see her. As I hope never to see her again!"

April felt as if all her features grew so taut they actually hurt her.

"It is most unfortunate, Don Carlos," she said, "that you introduced two alien influences to your ward, two young women from England! You should be more careful when it is of the utmost importance to you that she develops along the right lines, and you should certainly be more careful than you obviously have been when selecting someone to introduce to your friends as a future wife! A future wife—particularly if she has to influence Constancia!—should surely be without blemish?"

She realized that she was speaking with biting sarcasm, and that her tongue was running away with her, but she was unable to prevent herself. He looked so suave and condescending now that his anger had past, and even the humorous gleam in his eyes did nothing to soften her feeling of resentment. In fact it increased it, for she should not forget the way Doña Igniatia's glance had travelled over her in the *patio,* as if she was indeed an alien influence, and there was little or nothing that could be done about her.

"If your plans for Constancia are so important," April rattled on, "why didn't you tell me about her when you asked me to marry you? When you insisted I'd *have* to marry you!" correcting herself in some confusion.

"You put it rather crudely," Don Carlos said, his expression suddenly grave. "The circumstances under which I proposed to you were unfortunate, but I think you can forget that there was any necessity for my proposal. The reason why I said I shall not rush you into marriage was because I think it is only right that you should have an opportunity to get to know me."

"Thank you," she said, her expression scarcely altering. "But we were talking about Constancia. It doesn't seem that I shall be a good influence for her..."

"That is nonsense," he declared, lighting himself a cigarette. "There is no reason at all why you should not be a very good influence. You are not very many years older than she is, and the one thing she has always lacked is young companionship. My sister has done her best for her for years, but Ignatia has never married, and her ideas of the life young people should lead nowadays are, perhaps, a little out of date. Nevertheless, she is an excellent disciplinarian, and Constancia needs discipline. All young girls—in fact, all young things—need discipline."

April tightened her lips.

"That sounds to me somewhat barbaric."

He regarded her coolly.

"No doubt it does, when you were brought up in a country that neglects to discipline the young. But we are realists compared with you. We recognize the dangers ... you recognize them only when it is too late. Or very often too late!"

April looked down at her tightly linked hands.

"You mean," she said quietly, "that if I had been a young girl brought up in this country—someone like Constancia, for instance—*you* would not have been forced to marry me!"

"We get back to the same subject," he observed, his tone a little harsh. "And let it be clearly understood, I do not permit myself to be forced into anything. *Anything*, is that quite clear?"

"Then...?" She regarded him with faintly perplexed eyes.

He ground out the cigarette he had just lighted in an ash-tray at his elbow.

"And of another thing you may be certain. If you had not all the qualities I expect Constancia to have —and which I am certain she has!—then I would most certainly not have asked you to marry me. The Formera women measure up to a certain standard, and I would be the last to let my family down. Although it is true I took a risk when I asked you to marry me, I no longer have the slightest doubt that in actual fact I took no risk. You have everything Constancia will have when she eventually takes a husband, and the only difference between you is that she has been guarded carefully and you have not."

April felt the slow colour rise to her cheeks. So they were back again at Constancia, and Constancia had everything! Then why didn't he marry her himself? Since he was so cold-blooded about this business of marrying, and at least he was devoted to Constancia! Possibly much more so than he realized!

She tried to subdue the turmoil inside her—partly resentful, partly concerned—and asked:

"And have you any plans for a future husband for Constancia? As Spanish girls mature much more quickly than we do in England——" with a decided edge to her voice, "it shouldn't be very long now before you are making arrangements for her wedding!"

She studied her lightly polished nails as she spoke, and then looked upwards quickly at Don Carlos. As she had expected, his face assumed a mask-like expression.

"There is no hurry for Constancia's marriage," he said curtly.

"You have no man in view?"

He frowned.

"To say that would not be entirely truthful, but I do not wish her to marry yet."

"Then there is... someone? Your half-brother, Rodrigo, would seem to be a likely choice. I know they're inclined to fight now, but——"

119

She was not prepared for the violence of his reply, or the fierceness of the way he interrupted her.

"Rodrigo is not for Constancia! Understand that! If she marries anyone, it will most certainly not be my half-brother!"

"If she marries anyone...? But surely you *intend* that she shall marry someone?"

He stood up, thrusting back his chair so that it grated on the floor of the arbour. He looked so tall, and aloof, and hostile standing above her that April rose too, and without taking her arm he started to lead the way back to the house. The night was descending with a rush, and it was very dark in the ilex-bordered path, and she stumbled a little behind him.

"If you please, we will not discuss Constancia," he said in remote tones. "Her future is something that rests with me entirely, and therefore I prefer not to make it a subject for open discussion." He suddenly realized that he was striding ahead of her much too fast, and he paused to politely offer her his arm. But she declined it.

"Thank you, but I find that I walk better alone in these narrow ways," she said, and the coolness and clearness of her voice caused him to glance at her for an instant in the light of the first stars. Then, as it was his instinct to be chivalrous and protective, he fell back and walked a little behind her.

April tried hard not to stumble again as she forged ahead, and she tried even harder not to loathe the very thought of Constancia.

CHAPTER X

DINNER that night was not such a formal affair as it usually was, for Rodrigo refused to be formal. He was a young man with quite an attractive personality as well as the most engaging looks, and although slightly in awe of his half-brother—who, incidentally, was his employer as well—he was not in the least in awe of Ignatia, whom he teased quite openly at times, just as he teased Constancia. But his teasing of Constancia had a different note from that which predominated in his teasing of his half-sister.

Constancia was a very lovely young woman indeed when she was dressed in one of the expensive frocks with which her wardrobe was obviously very full. Mostly they were dark dresses, of lace or silk. But there was one that flamed like the short skirt in which she rode pillion behind her guardian, and another of delicate cream lace which lent her the look of an exquisite cream-coloured rose, especially as she nearly always wore roses, or a gardenia, in her hair.

Ignatia went in for heavy satins and velvets, in which she must have felt very warm on airless Andalusian nights. But she always looked remarkably cool and composed as she sat facing her brother at the opposite end of the long dining table.

April was the one who felt shabby and out of it, and she made up her mind that the next time she went into one of the larger towns she would buy herself a few additions to her wardrobe.

After her conversation with Don Carlos on the

terrace she had hardly bothered about what she wore, but Rodrigo's eyes told her he found her very satisfying to gaze at. In the big *sala,* before dinner, he had been most attentive, putting a glass of sherry into her hand before Don Carlos could possibly reach her, and inviting the displeasure of his brother by taking up his position beside her on the damask-covered settee and commencing a conversation with her that excluded every one of the others.

On any other night Don Carlos might have revealed his displeasure—indeed, April was becoming quite adept at recognizing the signs of rising displeasure in her fiancé, and not least amongst them was the cold flash of the dark eyes, and an uncompromising setting of the lines of his handsome mouth—but tonight he seemed too preoccupied to be aware of very much that was going on around him. He had an unusually gentle smile for Constancia, when she made her appearance, as if he was forgiving her for the incident of the afternoon, and he was gravely courteous to his sister. But April had the feeling that he looked through her whenever his eyes turned in her direction, and Rodrigo he merely humoured occasionally.

At least, until they were halfway through dinner, when he caught his brother looking very earnestly at Constancia, and the girl flushed. Flushed quite unmistakably.

Don Carlos spoke sharply.

"You will not return from Madrid until you have news for me, Rodrigo? I wish this business to be settled without the necessity for a second visit."

"I promise you I will do my best," Rodrigo assured him, the sudden intentness fading from his expression, and his look shifting to April. He sprang up to pull out her chair for her as she rose to leave the table, and then he held open the door of the dining *sala* for the ladies to leave.

"It is a fine night, *señorita*," he whispered to April. "While Carlos is attending to some papers I have to take with me tomorrow, may I show you the garden?"

She was about to reply that she knew the garden very well by this time, but Don Carlos spared her the necessity. Behind her she heard him thrust back his chair at the table and come after them, and as soon as he spoke she knew that the liqueurs and cigars would be ignored for once.

"You are somewhat over-attentive, Rodrigo," he remarked with dry curtness. "I wish your co-operation in the library. You will come with me?"

And Rodrigo had no option but to go with him.

Two mornings later Carlos took her to lunch at the house of one of his numerous relatives, an elderly aunt, who lived in a good deal of state nearby. She too had a house in Madrid, and she took it for granted that April knew all about the alterations and improvements to Don Carlos's house, and she talked of little else during the long-drawn-out lunch in a somewhat oppressive dining *sala*. She was plump and affable, and not in the least like Doña Ignatia, but April had the feeling that she was even more surprised than Doña Ignatia because her nephew was to marry a young Englishwoman he appeared to know very little about.

She pumped April in a quiet way about her background when the meal was over, and they were sipping coffee in a shuttered main *sala*, with the fans whirring, but Don Carlos came to his fiancée's rescue and explained that she was an orphan, and her father had been a clergyman. He said nothing about the way in which they met—and April certainly didn't expect him to do so—and Doña Amalia made sympathetic noises, and said how sad a thing it was to be a member of a small family.

"But when you marry Carlos you will be one of us," she added complacently. She looked with pride at her nephew. "He is the recognized head of our family, and we all look to him for guidance in all our affairs. I cannot imagine what life would be like without someone so tolerant and capable to advise and direct."

"Flattery, Tia Amalia," Don Carlos accused her, with an affectionate smile in his eyes, "will get you nowhere."

She patted his arm with her plump hand, white as all Spanish women's hands were white—whether young or elderly.

"Then in that case there is nowhere that I wish to go. I am happy having you look in upon me sometimes, remembering when I am not so well and sending me the little things that cheer me ... books I cannot choose myself, and always such qualities of flowers and fruit! And now you bring me this young lady who is to be your wife. It is a surprise, but a pleasant one!"

She beamed benignly at April.

Outside, Carlos apologized to April in case she had been bored.

"I'm sorry you had to listen to so much eulogizing, but old ladies become very repetitive. And Tia Amalia is a very fond old aunt."

April, who was glad there had been no mention of

124

Constancia—not even many inquiries about Ignatia —and no overwhelming surprise because a nephew who might have married almost anyone was marrying an unknown girl and thrusting her upon his family without warning, admitted truthfully:

"I liked her. She is obviously very devoted to you."

"As to that," he replied, as he took her arm lightly, in the manner he had, and guided her towards the car, "I am very devoted to her. She is perhaps the easiest of my relatives to get along with, and for that reason I decided she must be one of the first to meet you. She makes few inquiries, and is content to accept things as they are. I thought I would introduce you gradually to all the people that I know here, most of whom have known me all my life, and for that reason I have not so far encouraged Ignatia in her desire to give a big dinner party to introduce you. But Constancia has a birthday very soon, and we could give a party for that occasion."

April arranged the skirt of her gown carefully as she got into the car.

"You mean make it a double event?"

"Yes."

She studied his face carefully as he drove, his dark, slightly hawk-like features outlined by the brilliance of the afternoon, his black hair very black against the blueness of the sky. His hands rested lightly on the wheel, his shoulders were broad and relaxed, there was an aura of calmness and concentration about him.

He puzzled her acutely.

"Constancia will be seventeen on her birthday?"

"Yes." He smiled through the windscreen at the

road ahead, bordered by houses with flat roofs and
blank walls, so like Arab houses that it needed the gay
confusion of their gardens, their intricate wrought-iron
entrance gateways and the inevitable cascade of flowers above the gateways to identify them with the
Spanish soil in which they were set. "It is difficult to
believe that she is growing up so fast, but it is certainly something that one cannot ignore. And so important a birthday as a seventeenth birthday will have to
be marked in a special fashion."

"Of course." But April was thinking of her own
seventeenth birthday, when already her father's health
was failing, and somehow the occasion had gone un-
marked. But she was fully prepared to admit that a
seventeenth birthday was an important birthday. "So
you plan to give a dinner party?"

"Not just an ordinary dinner party. We can have
that as well, but I do think some other form of celebration is called for as well. Constancia will look for
it, and I'm afraid I have always humoured her."

April also stared through the windscreen, but her
expression was considerably more thoughtful than
his.

"In that case we'll have to give the matter a lot of
thought."

He glanced at her sideways.

"I would appreciate it if you would give it a lot of
thought. What do you do in England when a young
girl is seventeen?"

"We invite her friends ... her closest friends. And
sometimes we arrange a small dance."

He frowned.

"That would hardly satisfy Constancia. It will have
to be on a more impressive scale than that."

126

"Then you could give a really big dance ... a formal affair. Something in the nature of a ball and she could be the belle of it. If that would coincide with Spanish ideas of what is correct."

"It would, but I have already explained to you that it is to be a double-purpose affair. It is to introduce you—to celebrate our engagement!—as well as to proclaim Constancia's emergence from young girlhood. For in this country seventeen really is a marriageable age."

"Why not concentrate on Constancia?" she suggested.

He glanced at her much more sharply.

"Why?"

"Because it is Constancia's birthday that is of real importance. Our engagement isn't even very real ... or it has never seemed so to me!"

"I see," he exclaimed, and if she had been looking at him she would have seen that his mouth was set, and his eyes assumed an expression that might have puzzled her very much indeed.

But they were driving into the courtyard of the Formera home, and Constancia herself was waiting to watch them alight from the car, a very demure and delightfully dressed Constancia, holding a white lace parasol above her head, and wearing white lace gloves. Doña Ignatia had just emerged from the house behind her, and a chauffeur-driven car was waiting to take them out to tea with one of their numerous friends.

Doña Ignatia acknowledged the return of her brother and his fiancée with the coolest little bow and smile before she climbed into the car, but Constancia stood waiting with her parasol partially lowered to have a few words with her guardian.

"You had an enjoyable lunch? I am glad," she said, and smiled up at him with her melting, pansy-dark eyes ... and no two eyes could melt as swiftly, or as disarmingly, as hers did whenever she was near Don Carlos. Apart from that, in her girlish muslin with cherry red flowers embroidered all over it, and cherry red ribbons streaming from her hat, she had all the appeal of a seventeen-year-old, combined with the added allure of a true beauty. One who was at her prime, for Spanish girls lose this sort of beauty swiftly, and are often over-mature in their twenties.

Don Carlos put her into the car with a tenderness that suggested he was handling Dresden china.

"You, too, have a good time," he said, watched the car slip under the arch, and then turned back to April as if he had forgotten entirely her somewhat disconcerting observation about their engagement. Or it should have been disconcerting to him.

But apparently it was nothing of the kind!

Constancia made no attempt to cement a friendship with April, or even to lay the foundations of one. She was polite every time they came face to face, and encouraged by her guardian she talked English with April, and occasionally asked questions about England, and the way of life over there. She took a certain amount of interest in April's English-made clothes and shoes, her hair-style—which she once attempted to copy, although the effect was too dishevelled to be attractive—and her make-up. Doña Ignatia permitted her to use only lipstick, but as her skin was naturally deliciously creamy, and her eye-lashes required no beautifying treatment whatsoever, this was more than enough.

Nevertheless, there was a faint glitter of envy in her eyes sometimes when she watched April's soft hair swaying gently on her neck, and studied the way in which the faint touch of eye-shadow which she used in the evenings emphasized the depth and brilliance of her eyes. April's eyelashes were light brown, and she had to darken them a little, but her make-up was so discreet that even Doña Ignatia could take no exception to it.

She had several attractive linen frocks in her outfit, frocks that were severely simple in the way they were made, and Constancia expressed a wish to acquire linen frocks. Slacks represented a topic that was taboo, and April put hers away and was careful never to refer to them.

"But there's no reason why we shouldn't go shopping together some time, is there?" she suggested. "You have so many charming dresses I shouldn't think you need very much, but I could advise you about daytime dresses and cardigans," having observed the way Constancia had admired the one or two pastel-tinted sweaters she had appeared in. "We do rather go in for that sort of thing in England. Scottish knitwear, you know!"

This seemed to puzzle Constancia, who had heard of Scotland but never visited it; but in the end she shrugged her shoulders and returned ungraciously:

"Thank you, but Doña Ignatia advises on most of my clothes, and when I require something special she orders it for me. Of course, when we are in Madrid we do a lot of shopping, but Seville is too provincial to be

129

smart. The dress that I am to wear for my birthday celebration is to be ordered from Paris."

She sounded as if that was the final triumph.

"How nice," April commented, trying hard not to show any offence, and to be as patient as she knew how. "Not many young girls of your age have their dresses bought for them in Paris. You are lucky!"

"Yes, I am, aren't I?" Constancia agreed complacently. "But that is the way it has always been. Carlos is so good, so kind, and he can deny me nothing. He never has been able to do so!"

"Then you really are fortunate," April offered another comment, "to have such a generous guardian."

Constancia glanced at her obliquely under her thick eyelashes as she swayed to and fro in a hammock that was swung in a cool corner of the *patio*, beside a thick hedge of hibiscus. She had been riding her fiery Andalusian horse before breakfast, and she was still wearing her short scarlet skirt and polished boots. A gaudy neckerchief encircled her shapely throat, and her hair was in the tangle it often was at this hour.

"Perhaps you find it difficult to understand why Carlos should be so very generous to me? Why he can never say 'no' when I coax him enough!" Her eyes smiled. "He loved my mother!"

April flinched.

"Her portrait hangs in the house in Madrid. It is in Carlos's own study. You will see it when we go to Madrid."

April said nothing.

"She was very beautiful, and that is why the portrait remains where it is. I do not think you will be able to persuade him to have it removed."

"I have no intention of influencing Don Carlos about your mother's portrait," April told her, with so little expression in her voice that the other stared at her.

"You have not? But most women would be jealous... a Spanish woman would be jealous!" Her eyes grew contemptuous. "But you are English, aren't you? And Rodrigo says the English are a cold people! I would never permit another woman's portrait to hang in the house of my husband... I would tear it down with my own hands!" She looked as if she was capable of doing that very thing, and taking a venomous delight in it. And then the complacence returned to her expression, and she smiled—the smile of a born coquette. "But I am beautiful, like my mother. Don Carlos is aware of how beautiful I am... don't you think so, *señorita*?"

Doña Ignatia rustled across the floor of the *sala* in one of her stiff silk dresses, and she called to Constancia to go to her room at once and change out of her riding clothes. Constancia went, as if she was aware that she had scored a bulls-eye, and was leaving a certain amount of secret turmoil behind her.

Don Carlos asked April whether she wished to attend the cocktail party to which both Lady Hartingdon and her daughter had invited them, and when she said lethargically that it didn't very much matter to her whether they went or not he made up her mind for her.

"We will go," he said, looking at her rather shrewdly. "We will go, and we will take Constancia. It will be good for her also."

"If you think it will be good for Constancia, then by all means let us go."

She was unaware that her voice was dry.

He looked at her even more shrewdly.

"It is you I am thinking of," he told her. "It is natural that you should sometimes wish to be amongst people who are of your own kind, and who speak your language. The fact that I speak it doesn't give me an English type of mind," smiling a little oddly.

That was true, she thought, gazing at him. He saw her eyes widen.

"Any more than the fact that you are rapidly acquiring Spanish gives you a Spanish type of mind!"

That was very true, also, and her eyes grew wider still. She couldn't help wondering just how different he was from an Englishman of the same age, and with the same experience of life, and whether they ever thought the same thoughts, and had the same sort of secret desires. Whether his mind and hers were utterly dissimilar. Whether *they* ever thought the same thoughts!

He smiled again, even more oddly.

"All men are alike under the skin!" he murmured, proving he could read her mind, "or so we are told! But you don't necessarily have to believe it!"

Then as he saw her colour delicately he took her hand and surprised her by kissing it.

"We will go, shall we?" he said softly. "We will go to the Hartingdons? And perhaps Señorita Jessica will have some ideas we can adapt for Constancia's birthday celebration. I have decided a formal dinner will be much better for the announcement of our engagement!"

CHAPTER XI

The formal dinner took place less than a week later, and the Hartingdon cocktail party preceded it by a couple of days.

The Hartingdon house was typically Spanish, but it was filled with some very beautiful English furniture. Sir James Hartingdon was such a lover of Spain and the Spanish way of life that he would have been quite prepared to dispense with English chintzes, flowery carpets that merely attracted the moth, and comfortable English suites of furniture with deep cushions and yielding springs. But Lady Hartingdon wouldn't have been happy for a moment without her afternoon tea and her lace-edged tray-cloths, family photographs crowded together on occasional tables, and a dining-room sideboard stacked with silver.

Sir James was a very charming man, who had forgotten what it was like to live in England, but had served his country well abroad. He enjoyed meeting people—all sorts of people—and he enjoyed meeting April very much indeed. He told Don Carlos he was highly delighted that he was marrying one of his own countrywomen, and although Lady Hartingdon didn't altogether echo his enthusiasm she smiled bleakly at April, and Jessica smiled less bleakly, but with a heartiness that was undoubtedly a trifle forced.

She was wearing a striking cocktail dress of emerald brocade, and an arresting emerald bracelet flashed on her wrist. It was just possible it was not real, but it drew attention to the excellent shape of her forearm, the whiteness of her skin, and her long-fingered hands.

Constancia, who was wearing one of her demure dresses with a lot of white frilling at the neck, had a special smile for Jessica as soon as she saw her. It was a grateful smile, as if she was quite sure she owed her invitation to her, and she was in any case a keen admirer of Sir James Hartingdon's daughter.

From conversations April had gathered that Jessica had displayed a lot of interest in Constancia, and the two often rode together, and went on shopping expeditions together. The unfortunate violet slacks had been bought during one of these expeditions.

Now Constancia edged as close to Jessica as she could, although several young men were endeavouring to surround her, and keep her isolated from the rest of the room. It was a very big room, and a lot of people helped to fill it, and a lot more people overflowed on to the terrace and the cool lawns outside it. Sir James employed a positive team of gardeners, and his lawns were as green as they might have been in England, while the scent of his roses was like a kind of incense.

Most of the guests were Spanish, and they stood or sat about in groups, looking rather solemn, as they usually did do on public occasions. There were several pretty girls like Constancia—although not one was as lovely as she was—a number of matrons and elderly men, and a mere handful of younger men. And most of the younger men were congregated about Jessica.

She didn't flirt with them, but her smile and her looks seemed to hold them captivated. Shy fiancées who wouldn't have dared to exchange more than a nod and a smile with members of the opposite sex who were not doomed (or looking forward) to marrying them sat with their chaperones in the laps of the huge chesterfields and sipped innocuous glasses of lemonade while the only beings of any interest to them behaved like moths irresistibly attracted to a candle, and the candle—until Don Carlos arrived with April and Constancia—was Jessica.

Then the interest shifted—not so noticeably that she could take offence—and April felt herself the cynosure of many pairs of dark, masculine eyes, just as she had sometimes done in Madrid. Her soft brown hair, swinging on slender shoulders, provided them with a distraction that was also a novelty, and they gravitated slowly towards her, waiting for Don Carlos to present her, which he did after he had presented her to all the dowagers and the younger women.

April's dress was clear lime green, and her accessories were all white. Her hat was shady, and there was a single white flower nestling under the brim, which lent her a touchingly youthful look. Don Carlos's ring showed through the fine nylon gloves she wore, and as she held out her hand many pairs of eyes dropped to it... but these were feminine eyes.

Don Carlos had been the catch of the district, but now he was caught, and the women were all filled with a burning curiosity. In the hearts of many mamas there must have been a burning vexation, also, and perhaps that accounted for much of the stiffness April sensed in the women. The men, without exception, were all charming to her, although they dared not do more than look their admiration with Don Carlos keeping so close to her side that every time she moved she felt his sleeve brush against her bare arm, and frequently his cool fingers were underneath her elbow.

His attitude was possessive, even if his expression gave away nothing at all, and April had the feeling that practically every woman in the room envied her either a little or a great deal. And the thought crossed her mind that, if she were what every woman there imagined her to be (with the possible exception, that is, of Jessica Hartingdon, was was not the type to be easily deceived, and Constancia, who was too close to her guardian to be deceived)—if she was a happy bride-to-be, waiting impatiently for the day when she became the Don's wife, and had every reason to anticipate happiness as his wife—then she would indeed be someone to arouse envy.

But as it was, every time he said, "This is Miss Day, who is to become my wife," she winced inwardly. Winced, and longed to be able to know that one day she would be, in very truth, his wife! For it was no good deceiving herself ... it hadn't taken her long to overcome the antagonism his autocratic ways had at first aroused in her, and that coldness and hardness she believed to be part of him were all part of a deadly charm that had ensnared her as if she was a rabbit caught in an actual snare. Each time she felt his fingers brush against the slightly moist flesh of her upper arm—for it was very hot, and the fans in the room didn't make much difference to the temperature, with so many people collected together—she felt as if an electric spark was generated, and a tiny, tingling shock sped along all the sensitive nerves of her body, as well as right down to the tips of her fingers.

But he remained cool and remote, smiling at her,

fetching her a drink with ice chinking in it and lots of revivifying lime, placing her in a chair in a shady corner of one ̦of the lawns when the heat and the conversation—the effort to appear completely normal, and completely happy—overcame her to such an extent that she turned pale, and had to beg him in a whisper to take her out into the air and away from everyone for a short while.

The corner of the garden to which he led her was beautifully secluded, and roses formed a bower that added to their seclusion, and scented the air with their perfume. April drew in deep breaths of it, gulping it down into her lungs—that and the cool breath from the sea, that was growing cooler with the slipping of the sun towards the west—and Don Carlos stood beside her and looked down at her with an anxious expression on his face.

All his remoteness and his detachment had gone, and his dark eyes were alive with concern as he studied her.

"You are better now?" he asked. "That room was very hot, and it is far too overfurnished for our climate ... but Sir James prefers it that way. He likes to live in Spain and keep a little corner of England alive in his heart as well! Or Lady Hartingdon does."

Perhaps, one day, April thought, I too ... !

And then she looked into his face as he dropped into a chair beside her, felt her heart do a kind of somersault at the extent of the anxiety she recognized in his eyes, and the unusual softness of his mouth. Such a devastatingly handsome mouth, and when it was not smiling a little grimly, or a trifle mockingly. When she found that she couldn't drag her eyes away from it, and her heart thumped wildly ... Then she knew that there were circumstances under which she could live in Spain for the rest of her life—live anywhere, away from all familiar things, and be divinely happy, if...

If...? But it was a big "if"! If he was beside her always, and he loved her, instead of merely wanting her to be his wife for some reason that she couldn't properly understand! If that suddenly tender mouth, instead of kissing the back of her hand, lightly and gracefully, as it frequently did, might one day draw close to hers and fill her with utter ecstasy as he kissed her, as every woman yearns to be kissed by the man she loves!...

And suddenly the thought of being loved by Don Carlos was so overwhelming that, instead of recovering her normal colour, she turned even paler.

"I will take you home!" he exclaimed instantly. "You really are not well!"

But she assured him that she was perfectly well. She took a firm grip of herself—averted her eyes from him—and the colour came seeping back into her cheeks, and then started to burn them, and the whole of her throat and brow, as the utmost confusion replaced the wild longings of a moment before.

"Nevertheless, I think I will take you home," Don Carlos said, as if he was perturbed by her changing mood, her fluctuating colour. "I will collect Constancia, and we will all three make our *adieux*."

Constancia had been introduced by Jessica to a young Englishman who was staying temporarily in the district, and although she was normally shy in the presence of any man who was not either her guardian or Rodrigo, she seemed to be getting along very well with him. He was a young artist, who was travelling through Spain, and he was staying temporarily with the Hartingdons. He was some sort of cousin of Jessica's, and he had a tinge of her red in his hair, but his eyes were blue instead of the strange sort of jade green that hers were.

It was quite obvious that his artistic eye appreciated Constancia very much indeed, and although she had started the day in a slightly sullen mood she was laughing and displaying her perfect little white teeth, and her eyes had a velvety brilliance about them when Don Carlos returned to collect her, with April, looking more like herself, accepting the support of his arm.

Constancia's eyes lost their laughing look when she saw the way in which April's fingers reposed in the crook of her guardian's arm, and when she saw the sudden frown of displeasure on his face the sullen look returned.

"We are leaving, Constancia," he said curtly, as if the sight of her behaving in a natural manner with a young man who was not even her own countryman displeased him. "April is unwell, and I am taking her home."

Constancia did not answer, but her lower lip pouted and the look she darted at April was hardly one of sympathy.

"Oh, what a pity!" Jessica exclaimed, looking rather curiously at April, but also refraining from pouring out sympathy. She introduced her cousin, and the young man bowed gallantly over April's hand. "We have been putting our heads together and trying to think up something unusual for Constancia's birthday ... an unusual way of celebrating it, I mean. And I suggested a trip somewhere."

"Oh, yes?" Don Carlos murmured politely. "But it does not strike me that a trip is a very good way of celebrating a birthday."

"I was thinking of Granada," Jessica admitted. "Mark has been staying there recently, and painting the Alhambra. In fact, he has painted a whole series of pictures, and they've fired me with enthusiasm to have another look at Granada myself—before," she added, with an oblique glance at the Spaniard, "I go home in a few weeks' time. Constancia doesn't seem to have been taken there very recently, Miss Day has probably never seen it, and it might be a good idea to make up a party and stay a night at an hotel. We could have a special dinner, and dance afterwards. That would be a real birthday celebration."

"Would it?" Don Carlos said sceptically, plainly anxious to be gone. "I think not!" And then, as Constancia's face dropped, and she looked at him pleadingly: "Who would make up this party?"

"Yourself, of course," Jessica replied swiftly, looking at him under her thick eyelashes, "and, naturally, Miss Day, Constancia, Rodrigo, Mummy and myself ... although I hardly think Daddy would consider it. He's not fond of driving two or three hundred miles nowadays, just to see the sights. And Doña Ignatia might not care for the drive, either. But Mark ... Mark would be willing to make up our numbers."

Mark smiled into Constancia's eyes, and agreed with the utmost fervour that he would be very willing to make up their numbers.

Don Carlos looked even less inclined to agree to the plan, and it was probably because Constancia smiled back at the Englishman. April could have warned him that no man who appeared in the least eager to win the favours of Constancia would be in the least likely to find favour with her guardian, and she also experienced a wry twinge because she was fairly certain she knew the reason.

The only thing she was not certain about was just how widely awake to the true nature of his attachment for Constancia Carlos himself was. And she wondered whether he made very big efforts to deceive himself ... herself being linked up with one of those efforts!

"In any case, we have at least a couple of weeks before we need make a decision about Constancia's birthday," he said. "And she might think of something herself that will please her long before that."

But Constancia assured him she had already made up her mind.

"I wish to go to Granada," she said, and April wondered whether the look she gave him—compounded of childish coaxing, a faint touch of pleading, feminine witchery, and something much more arch .. perhaps a hope that she was woman enough to influence him, dear enough to make it impossible for him to refuse her, and feline enough to be intrigued by the possibilities of arousing his purely masculine jealousy—was a deliberately calculated look to break down his resistance.

Anyway, it made April feel suddenly sick, and Don Carlos turned away abruptly.

'We will see," he said, his tone unyielding, although his words were rather more than a half-promise ... an indication, in fact, that she had the power to win.

April saw the triumphant smile that flashed into Constancia's eyes.

The dinner party, two nights later, at which her betrothal to Don Carlos was formally announced, was even more of an ordeal for April.

Doña Ignatia was a wonderful hostess, and when preparing for an important event she undertook many of the tasks that, in other households, might have been deputed to servants. She personally inspected every piece of silver and every glass that found its way to the long, polished dining table. The lace table mats and the crystal finger bowls were placed in position by her long white fingers, and the arrangement of the flowers took her so long that April offered to help. But Doña Ignatia smiled at her politely and declined any assistance. She added a white gardenia to the bowl in the centre of the table, placed bowls of roses at each end of the table, set a single gardenia at each lady's place card, and then gathered up her refuse and departed with it to the kitchen, where she devoted another lengthy period to inspecting the contents of refrigerators and side tables.

Before she left the dining *sala* she suggested to April that she went upstairs and commenced her dressing, and April took the hint that she was in the way and climbed the handsome baroque staircase to her suite of rooms in a corner of the large white villa. Her dress for the evening had already been laid out over the bed, and it was the pale pink crêpe that she had once despised because it had cost so little. But tonight it would have to do, for she had had no opportunity to do any real shopping, and in Madrid she had been afraid to make inroads on her money for a really expensive evening gown, or anything at all that was expensive.

She looked like a wild rose when the dress was on, however, and it was wonderful what the soft lighting effects did for the dress itself. No one would be deceived into thinking it a creation, but the colour—like the inside of a shell, or the heart of a china rose—was infinitely kind to golden-brown hair and a complexion with which few people could find fault.

April brushed her hair until it shone as if moonbeams were caught up in the brightness of it, and she creamed her skin more thoroughly, perhaps, than she had ever creamed it in her life, and then added a touch of astringent lotion. The hot nights tended to make one perspire, and although she had never participated in an interminably long Spanish dinner to which large numbers of guests were invited, she had witnessed their effect on Venetia Cortez when she was acting hostess at just such a dinner party. She had frequently rushed into her bedroom with the perspiration shining on the tip of her nose, and her elaborate hair-style damp and flattened on her brow.

"Give me a simple three-course meal," she had declared, flicking powder all over her face, and using a perfume spray wildly. "These Spanish dinners go on half the night!"

So when April descended to the ground floor of the house, shortly before nine o'clock, she was prepared to be exhausted, and prepared to face up to her second real ordeal since becoming engaged to Don Carlos.

Although she sometimes thought that the ordeal of making the acquaintance of the members of Don

Carlos's family—on the female side— was the biggest ordeal she had yet undergone.

There was no one about, and she wandered through the quiet rooms. They smelled heavily of flowers, and underlying the flower perfume was the scent of beeswax. There was a swish of satin skirts on the stairs, and Ignatia joined her, looking as if she had done nothing all day but rest and prepare herself for the evening ahead of her, and had not recently had a somewhat tiresome interview with the cook, who had failed to carry out some of her instructions to the letter. She eyed April carefully, then told her she looked very nice.

"That is a charming dress," she murmured, but from her expression April could not make up her mind whether she meant it or not. She never did know where she was with Ignatia, whether she approved of her or otherwise, whether she resented the thought of her brother's marriage with a comparative stranger ... an unknown alien girl with no background whatsoever! Or whether, on the other hand, she thought it a good thing for her brother to marry, even if he had to pick on a stranger.

Rodrigo was the first of the guests to arrive, and he looked very handsome in his dinner jacket. He helped himself to a carnation in the hall and attached it to his buttonhole, and when he greeted his sister and bowed in front of April he was smiling and debonair.

Then Constancia came gliding into the *sala,* young and exquisite in pure white silk, and she had a string of lustrous pearls about her slender throat. For once she was not wearing any flowers, but she had never looked more beautiful. April felt her breath catch as

144

she gazed at her, and a small ache of envy made her throat feel tight and uncomfortable for a moment.

For although she knew that she herself was quite attractive—she was too modest to rate her appeal for the opposite sex as any higher than that—she could never compare with Constancia. With those glorious dark, melting eyes, those breathtaking eyelashes that fluttered nervously when she looked demurely down at her feet, that perfect skin that flushed so easily and divinely, and her arresting red mouth.

Even Rodrigo, his eyes prepared to mock at her when she entered the room, grew grave and thoughtful—as April had seen him do once before—when she acknowledged his presence with the merest little half-curtsy. She looked up at him with a smile, her ripe lips curving over her faultless teeth, her eyelashes fluttering a little.

"You had a good time in Madrid?" she inquired, and for a moment he didn't reply.

"It was not unamusing," he returned at last, and she sent him a more calculated look between her thick eyelashes. "But I am quite glad to be back," he added.

Don Carlos entered the room, and Constancia instantly forgot all about Rodrigo, and dropped a curtsy for the benefit of her guardian. He tweaked her ear, and then touched her cheek with the tip of a long forefinger.

"You are very charming, *cara*," he told her.

Her eyes glowed.

April felt his eyes rest upon her, but all she could think of was that he was comparing her dress with the super-elegance of the dresses worn by his sister and his ward. She wanted to stammer out an apology, that she

145

hadn't arrived at the house prepared for elegant occasions, but she realized in time how foolish that would be. How his eyebrows would ascend in mild surprise, and his sister's also. These people were used to elegant occasions, and were always prepared for them.

And Constancia would look down her little straight nose in delighted contempt if she made a *faux pas*.

The guests started to arrive in earnest, and after that it wasn't long before they went in to dinner. Don Carlos was displaying consideration for his English fiancée in curtailing the period devoted to sipping apéritifs and chattering in rapid Spanish in the big *sala*, and at dinner she found she was close to him, given the place of honour at his right hand.

Ignatia sat at the foot of the table, and Constancia was somewhere between Rodrigo and another young and admiring Spaniard. The dinner was an affair of many courses, all of them justifying Ignatia's insistence on collaborating closely with her cook, and champagne filled the glasses that sparkled before anything at all was poured into them. Afterwards. there were speeches and toasts, and then came the moment the whole dinner table was awaiting. The moment when the host stood up at the head of the flower-decked, glittering table, and made the announcement they had all heard already, but on this occasion was strictly formal.

"I would like you to drink to the health of my wife-to-be," he said, and April underwent a most curious experience. She ceased to be aware that there were other people in the room, and that everyone of them had his, or her eyes fixed upon her, and all she saw were the eyes of Don Carlos, as he lifted his glass high to her. He was looking down at her, a straight, tall,

146

commanding figure, impeccable in his evening things, and tonight he had a white rosebud in his buttonhole. It might have been an accident, but the finger of his free hand touched it as he called the toast.

"To you, *amada*," he said softly, as he sank into his seat again, and continued to hold her soft brown eyes with his velvety black ones. "To us both," he added, in so low an undertone that nobody else could possibly have overheard it, and touched her glass with his own. "Now drink, little one," he urged her, and removed the white rosebud from the front of his dinner jacket and laid it beside her plate. "That is for you to keep. It is wilting already, but press it in a book— do something with it!—only don't throw it away!"

His voice was light, and to the rest of the room it must have sounded bantering, but his eyes were deeper and darker than she had ever known them before with earnestness. As he put her champagne glass into her hand his fingers touched hers.

April felt as if a whole series of electric shocks sped up and down her arm, and her whole being was dissolved in wonder and delight. He had selected a white rosebud to wear in his buttonhole—what was that supposed to symbolize?—on the occasion of an announcement of a betrothal that should have meant nothing, and he had given the rosebud to her. He had charged her to keep it! Not to destroy it!

What did that mean?

Her brown eyes developed a light that must have dazzled him, it was so like that of a star peering at its reflection in limpid water, and her pale English complexion was suddenly suffused with rose ... the most revealing rose. She found it difficult to summon up a voice to answer him, and when she did it was the merest, shyest whisper, while she clutched at the rose-bud and wanted to hold it up against her face.

"Of course, if you ... if you want me to keep it! ..."

"I do."

The world rocked while he deliberately kept her glance chained to his, and in the dark depths of his eyes she saw so many things that she had never imagined she would see there. Urgency, a touch of tenderness, possessiveness ... a promise that set her heart pounding. And then, halfway down the table, Constancia created a diversion by turning as white as a sheet and letting out a choked gasp, as if she was about to faint.

"I ... You'll have to excuse me! ... Please!"

She stood swaying on her feet, clutching at the edge of the table, while her eyes looked tormented, and her scarlet lower lip started to bleed because she had torn at it ruthlessly with her hard little white teeth. She turned to Rodrigo imploringly, as if he was the only one who could possibly help her, and he rose to the occasion by leaping to his feet and catching her in his arms as she collapsed, a small white silk heap, against him.

She started to sob bitterly and wildly, and by that time the whole company was on its feet, and Don Carlos wrenched his extraordinarily revealing look away from April and strode down the length of the table to the further assistance of his ward. April heard her moan and let out a wild appeal to be permitted to retire to her room, Don Carlos said something firmly but soothingly, and a bewildered Rodrigo handed her over to him and he led her from the room.

Everyone present saw the tender way in which Carlos attempted to soothe his ward, and everyone heard her passionate stream of reproaches as he led her from the room.

"I hate her, I hate her!... I'll die if you really marry her!..."

Looks were exchanged, eyebrows weren't merely raised, they flew up, and Doña Ignatia, her expression quite unreadable, quietly left the table and went hastening after her brother and Constancia.

April, a nasty sick sensation at the base of her stomach, seized the opportunity while no one was looking at her to escape through the open french windows into the garden.

CHAPTER XII

SHE had no idea how long she wandered out there in the moonlight and the starshine, the soft, silken warmth, and all the heady scents of the garden, before Rodrigo found her, and apologized anxiously for his half-brother.

"You mustn't blame Carlos for leaving you alone like this! Constancia has been so spoiled. Our girls are not normally as spoiled as she is, and not many of them would behave as she did tonight. She gets so worked up..." His English was good, but in moments of stress it deserted him a little. "She has what you call a 'thing' about Carlos... that is, she has for him an affection..."

"I've been aware of that ever since I met her," April replied, with a good deal of dryness. "But it was rather inconsiderate of her, if her affection is very real, to upset him tonight, don't you think?"

Rodrigo agreed with her.

"Nevertheless, her affection is very real."

"Too real, would you say?" looking him straight in the eye. "The affection of a young girl for her guardian does not normally overcome her on occasions such as tonight, when he announces his engagment. Not to the extent that it overcame Constancia, anyway!"

Rodrigo agreed again. In the moonlight his dark

eyes were not particularly happy, and his handsome if rather weak mouth drooped at the corners.

April touched his sleeve.

"I'm sorry," she said gently, realizing suddenly that he had followed her not only to offer her some comfort, but to derive some comfort for himself. He and Constancia might fight together, might provoke one another with their eyes, provoke one another still more with ill-chosen words, but Rodrigo was very well aware of the charm of Constancia, the beauty of her. It was a stormy sort of beauty that matched his own deep and slightly stormy eyes, and together—such a very handsome pair—they should have been very happy if there was no Don Carlos.

But for Constancia Don Carlos had been the most important thing in her life since she was a child, and she knew that her mother—whom she so closely resembled—had been the dearest thing in life to him. If she had grown up with the idea—the secret aspiration—of replacing her mother in his heart one day she was not entirely to be blamed, for there were not many men who revealed their affection for a ward as Carlos de Formera y Santos did. It was in his eyes whenever he spoke to her, his touch for her was especially tender. He refused to face up to the idea that she might marry one day.

And tonight he had been upset because she had been upset. April had caught a glimpse of his face before he left the dining *sala* with his arm about the weeping girl's shoulder, and the concern in it had almost startled her. It had certainly given her a lot to think about as she paced the garden paths.

"I'm sorry," she repeated, as Rodrigo's expression grew even more revealing. "I don't suppose it made you very happy to hear that outburst tonight, did it? Constancia probably didn't mean to hurt you at all, but she did hurt you, didn't she?"

He smiled crookedly.

"I've known her for years, and I think she ought to be spanked occasionally, but . . ." His expression grew wry. "One day I hope to marry her, and then perhaps I'll do a little spanking myself, but it may be too late! Carlos will not consider me as a future husband for Constancia, but if only he would I could handle her . . . I feel certain of that. She is not all fire and resistance . . . at least, not always. And it is high time she married."

"But she is very young," April demurred.

"She will be seventeen in two weeks' time, and at seventeen a young woman of Constancia's temperament is old enough for marriage. She needs a husband to discipline her, and I would do that." He was speaking very earnestly, and April refrained from smiling slightly at his choice of words. "She is like a young horse that needs to be broken in, and whereas Carlos would ruin her I would be good for her. In time we would be very happy," he concluded simply.

"Then why will not Carlos let you marry her?"

He looked at her closely, in the moonlight that was silvering her pale dress.

"You have not heard?" he asked quietly. "About her mother? Carlos would have married her, only she chose someone else."

"Yes, I know all about that," April admitted, a long sigh in the words. She was wondering whether she had allowed herself to be deceived at the dinner table, and those moments when Carlos looked at her with a whole world of meaning in his eyes had been moments that she imagined, and he had not intended that his eyes should convey anything at all to her.

And then something pricked her fingers, and she looked down to discover that she was still holding the rosebud, and although it was wilting fast it still had a delicate perfume which came up to her. Her heart started to beat faster.

"I—I suppose men forget disappointments of that sort in time?" she suggested, a sluggish hope lifting up its head, while she took a kind of delight in the feel of the rose thorn embedding itself in her flesh. "Women too, if . . . if that sort of thing happens to them."

"I'm afraid I can't help you there, *señorita*," Rodrigo told her, the wry twist clinging to the corners of his mouth. "I'm hoping I will not have to get over such a disappointment myself!"

"Of course." She looked up at him swiftly, sympathy and understanding throbbing in her voice. He was young—even younger than she was herself—but the hurt was just the same. Unrequited love is a painful pill to swallow, and judging by that night's exhibition he might have to gulp his down somehow or other. Just as she . . . but she had never even hoped that Carlos would love her. That would be too much to expect from a man who proposed as Carlos had proposed to her! For some reason that seemed good to him at the time, but had nothing to do with human emotions.

She tried to speak encouragingly to Rodrigo.

"Constancia is so very young that she is bound to turn to someone young in the end. Don Carlos has been good to her almost all her life, and naturally she clings to him. It is the clinging of a daughter to a parent!"

"Is it?" His dark eyes were very sober as he peered at her, and just a little cynical. "Do you see Carlos in the role of a parent to a young woman like Constancia? He is barely old enough to be her father. Her mother was several years older than he was when he conceived his infatuation for her, and today there is hardly a woman in Adalusia who would not be eager to marry him! You yourself, several years his junior, have consented to marry him! Then why should not Constancia hope that one day ... or shall we say she *hoped*, until tonight!"

April licked her lips.

"But she knows now that he is no longer free."

"Does she?" Cynicism fairly blazed in his eyes. "Then why did he permit her to make that scene without one word of rebuke? It was a scene—put on solely for his benefit!—and he left his guests to escort her to her room. He left you—to whom he had only just announced his betrothal!—to wander out here in the garden alone, while he undertook the task of quietening the hysterics of a tempestuous girl who, but for his consistent spoiling, might have known how to behave herself tonight!" His voice sounded intensely grim. "And apparently he is still with her, soothing her, reasoning with her, making half-promises to her ... or perhaps they are not half-promises!"

Then he caught a glimpse of April's expression in the moonlight, and he apologized softly.

"I'm so sorry, April, *cara!* I was forgetting that you ... that you really are betrothed to him!"

"It's all right," April said huskily. "I realize that you're upset."

154

"And you...?" He touched her arm gently. "You have every cause to be upset. All those women in there, with their upraised eyebrows and their tight little smiles, talking amongst themselves! Constancia really does deserve to be punished, for she has placed you in an intolerable position. Carlos must realize——"

But at that moment Carlos materialized at his elbow, and whatever he realized it did not prevent him from addressing his half-brother curtly and coldly.

"It was good of you to see to it that April was not entirely neglected, Rodrigo, but now you may safely leave her to me! I think it would be a good idea if you returned to the rest of my guests inside. They are now drinking coffee in the *sala.*"

Rodrigo looked almost rebellious for a moment, as if he wanted to accuse Carlos openly of pandering to the whims of Constancia to such an extent that she might one day be impossible to handle, but his brother's austere looks obviously caused him to change his mind, and he bowed to April and withdrew into the house.

Carlos offered his arm to his fiancée, and suggested that she might enjoy a further stroll in the moonlight.

"I have something to say to you, and it can be better said out of doors," he remarked.

April felt as if the muscles of her face had stiffened like the whole of her body, as she refused his arm and walked at his side and asked after Constancia.

"I hope she has recovered from her agitation at dinner. She does rather enjoy creating scenes, doesn't she?"

Don Carlos was silent for a moment, biting rather fiercely at his lower lip. And then he frowned.

"She is quite calm now," he admitted, in an expressionless voice. "She is attending to the ravages all those tears wreaked upon her appearance, but in a short while she will rejoin our guests. I have requested it."

April felt very much as Rodrigo was plainly feeling a minute or so before, seething with indignation but bereft of speech. A kind of impotence connected with her vocal chords.

"I regret that I had to leave the dinner table as abruptly as I did," Carlos observed.

April clenched her hands down at her sides.

"I have made up my mind that I can't possibly marry you, Don Carlos," she said stiffly—and, now that she thought about it, she had never yet called him simply "Carlos." "It would be ridiculous for you and me to think of marrying when there isn't the slightest reason why we should even contemplate it. And as for Constancia ... I'm sure she would be happier if you told her at once that——"

"I shall tell her nothing," Don Carlos said quietly, taking her arm very determinedly and leading her to the remote corner of the garden where they had talked once before. "I shall tell her nothing, and I'm going to ask you to look at that remarkable moon up there, and think how much larger and brighter it is than your cold English moon! I remember, when I was in England—and I was at school in England, you know, and I have paid it several visits since—I used to think the moon had shrunk when I saw it climbing into the sky above your quiet English fields. Over here in Andalusia we are accustomed to vivid contrasts, to bril-

156

liant moonlight, and sunlight that hurts sometimes... or it can hurt, if you are unwise enough to pay it little respect, and ignore our excellent rule about siesta, and so forth."

April stared up at the moon as if compelled, and, also as if compelled, she stood quite still beside him when they reached the white-painted garden seats that were arranged in the protection of the arbour. She heard him continue softly:

"There is so much that you have not yet seen that I wish to show you here in Spain ... in Andalusia! For, to us, Spain is Andalusia. The wine harvest, that will take place very soon now, the spring fair—the *Sevilla Feria*—that lasts three days, with *corridas* each afternoon and songs and *seguidillas* that go on until dawn. Cordova ... that is a lovely district, and was once an Arab settlement..."

"Yes, I know," she answered, as softly as he had spoken. "I've read about it."

He smiled and looked down at her shining hair, stirring softly in the night breeze, and brushing against his shoulder.

"And when did you read about Spain?" he asked. "Was it before you left England, or since you arrived here? Many of the books in my library will give you a lot of information about this country if you are interested."

"Oh, I am interested," she assured him. Her breath caught. The moon was exercising its magic, and she felt strangely excited. "But I did most of my reading about Spain before I left England. It was the reason why I wanted to come here and see it all for myself."

"And now that you are here do you feel the urge to go away again?"

She put back her head and looked up at him, and their eyes came together as if at a pre-arranged signal.

"No. No, I don't want to go away again... not back to England, where there is no one."

"You mean... no one belonging to you?"

"Yes."

The word was like a soft sigh, and he ran his hand down the smooth side of her throat, and then cupped her chin with it.

"But here I am! And in a short while you are going to marry me. So you will say no more about reasons for contemplating marriage! And you will remember that here in Spain is your future husband!" He stroked her cheek, then touched her hair almost wonderingly. "Oh, *amada*, why will you not believe that you and I can be so very, very happy?" he breathed, and lowered his mouth to hers. She gasped at the sweetness of it as his lips touched hers, and then she clung to him because her instincts cried out to her to do so, and even if her will had been strong enough she couldn't have resisted him.

The kiss went on and on, deeply satisfying—satisfying a need that had become an obsession... with her, at any rate. And Don Carlos's arms held her so closely that she might suddenly have become a part of him, her slim body pressed hard against him, her eager mouth responding rapturously to his. And then she heard him whisper again.

"*Amada, amada!*" He rested his cheek against her hair, and she felt the slight, exciting roughness of it, the deep beating of his heart against her slender ribs. "My little love, my pale flower." His voice was full of tenderness, and then he said quiveringly tender things to her in Spanish, and she wished she had a better grasp of his language, while the moonlit world swayed round her, the stars performed an eccentric dance, and but for his arms she might have fallen, for she was caught up in a giddy whirl of ecstasy that was unlike anything she had ever known before.

And then his arms slackened, she felt him draw away, and the ecstasy was dissolved in something quite ridiculous, something humiliating.

"Forgive me," he said, peering into the shadows at the end of the paved path which led to the secluded arbour, "but I thought I saw ... Constancia!" There was a vague blur of white at the end of the path, and beside it was a dinner-jacketed form. Don Carlos's whole body stiffened, and he put April quite finally away from him. But for the fact that she was feeling vague and bewildered she would have noticed how his nostrils suddenly flared, and his eyes flashed. His voice, however, was bleak enough to jerk her back to the harshness of reality when he spoke again. "It *is* Constancia! She promised to behave, and now she is wandering about the garden with Rodrigo. I will not have it! ..." This time she noticed the concentration of anger in his eyes, the tautness of his mouth. All tenderness had fled from him, and he was the Don Carlos she had first met in Madrid, icily angry because some people he had counted amongst his friends had behaved in a manner he could not approve ... a manner that was alien to his own code.

"Wait here," he said to April, and leaving her in the shadows of the summer-house he strode forward along the path until the two figures, startled by his approach, separated until there was at least a couple of feet between them.

159

"Go to your room!" Carlos ordered Constancia. "Go to your room and stay there!"

She gave one frightened glance up at him, and then fled in obedience to the order.

Rodrigo, left face to face with his half-brother, attempted for the second time that night to protest:

"This is too much! Carlos, you have no right——"

Carlos, towering above him, assured him that he had every right.

"Constancia is my ward. She does what I say! You, *amigo*, will be well advised to do what I say, also! Leave her alone, and as the hour is growing fairly late you may consider that you have done your duty here long enough. I suggest that you go home, and in the morning I will drive over and have a talk with you!"

Standing before the arbour, April watched and waited for Rodrigo to find the courage to defy his brother—the head of the House of Formera!—but it was quite obvious he hadn't the courage. Or the force of habit, and constant deference, was too much for him.

He turned on his heel and strode off along the path.

April experienced a strange revulsion of feeling. That night she had known a few minutes of astonished happiness while dinner was in progress, had suffered a nasty jolt and felt herself badly affronted and neglected when Carlos elected to devote himself to the task of soothing Constancia, and had apparently forgotten her existence for very nearly half an hour. Then, with his reappearance, she had forgotten resentment and tasted purest bliss, and now she was suddenly revolted by the proof she had been given that Constancia—and only Constancia!—could so affect the head of the House of Formera that he forgot everything—even an interval in the garden with his fiancée!—when something she did, or did not do, aroused emotions that were far more important than any other emotions.

In fact, everything else—everyone else—had no importance at all by comparison with the importance of Constancia!

April gathered up her skirts in her hands and ran blindly along a secondary path, back to the house which was blazing with light and the chatter of many people, to the seclusion of her own room.

CHAPTER XIII

For an hour or more she sat crouched in a chair by the window, half expecting him to come knocking on her door. She was well aware that this was a Spanish household, and even a fiancée's room was sacred at that hour of the night; but after those moments in the garden—that sudden release of feeling in ecstatic kisses—she felt that he must want to apologize, to explain.

But he did nothing of the sort, and April crept into bed at last feeling numb and unhappy, like a wounded creature. But even so she comforted herself with the thought that—in the morning—in the morning he *must explain*! He would say something about Constancia ... something that would throw light on his attitude towards her!

But again he did nothing of the kind, and when he met her after breakfast—and she always, nowadays, breakfasted in her room—in one of the broad verandas that flanked the central courtyard or *patio*, he merely looked at her very levelly, and inquired whether she had had a good night.

April wanted to gasp. She looked at him for a moment almost appealingly, and he hastened to place a chair for her with his usual impeccable politeness, and then he said something about the chaos after a dinner party. Apparently Ignatia had been making herself personally responsible for the clearing up of quite a lot of it, and she had been up at a fantastically early hour.

"Whatever she does, she does thoroughly," he said, "and, thanks to her, the party was, I believe, quite a success. But it was a pity you felt it necessary to retire to your room quite so early. I explained to our guests that you were indisposed."

April sat very still in her chair and studied him with amazement. That makes two of us, she thought! *Two of us so indisposed that we had to retire to our rooms!* Only Constancia had made a brief reappearance, before finally seeking sanctuary in her room!

April felt she wanted to laugh suddenly, hysterically... it was all quite fantastic! Don Carlos, in his finely tailored light grey suit, his Old Etonian tie, looking at her with a certain amount of undisguised reproach in his eyes, while his mouth was very cold. Cold and set like a steel trap; and unless one had had experience of the way that mouth could lift one to the heights of bliss... right up amongst the stars!

She trembled as her fingers grasped the rattan arms of her chair, and then she attempted to meet his eyes with a long, level look from her own brown ones. But the bleakness in his aroused a sensation like acute dismay.

"I'm sorry you had to... make apologies for me," she got out stiltedly.

He made a faint, shrugging movement with his shoulders—a coldly dismissing movement—and then walked to the veranda rail.

"I have agreed to the proposed plan for Constancia's birthday celebrations," he said, the brilliant morning sunshine making his features appear very harsh indeed. "Miss Hartingdon was unable to attend our dinner last night, but she sent a note reminding

163

me that, if the plan is to be put into action, arrangements must be made fairly soon. Hotels in the south are still fairly full, and we must make a reservation for our party. I have agreed to make the reservation myself, and to undertake all necessary arrangements for the outing."

"I see," April said.

He regarded her coldly.

"I am sure you will enjoy seeing Granada. It is one of the 'musts' on the lists of most visitors to our country. Such sights as the Alhambra are not quickly forgotten, and in the Generalife—which was the summer residence of our kings—there is the famous Courtyard of Lions. And there is much besides that you will no doubt find of interest."

He sounded as if he was quoting monotonously from a guide-book, and she wondered what had happened to the wooing voice—the throbbing, tender, masculine voice—that had described for her the charms of Andalusia only the night before.

Now she and he might be the completest of strangers, and it was impossible to believe that she had ever been held passionately close in his arms, and that he had called her his little love. She swallowed, and then started to wonder whether something had happened to her the night before that had led her to believe in happenings that never actually occurred.

She parted her lips to remind him, "I told you last night that I couldn't marry you! . . ." But somehow, in his present mood, and while he looked at her with such icy displeasure—as if she had committed a serious crime he found it hard to forgive—the words wouldn't leave her lips.

Instead, she heard herself say colourlessly:

"I'm sure I shall find it very interesting, but it's Constancia's birthday we will be celebrating. It's for her to enjoy it!"

From then until the day they left for Granada he behaved towards her as if they were the merest acquaintances—or she just an honoured guest in his house—and not betrothed to be married. Towards Constancia, on the other hand, he behaved with frequent and marked displays of affection, gentleness and indulgence, and she went about with a brighter smile on her face, and brighter eyes, than April had ever known her to have before. And whenever she looked at April there was an unmistakable gleam of triumph in her eyes.

Her birthday morning dawned with all the brilliance of an Andalusian morning at that season of the year, and they set off in two cars soon after a very early breakfast. Jessica had been right about Doña Ignatia, and she declined to accompany them, but Rodrigo had accepted the invitation with alacrity. They picked up Lady Hartingdon and her daughter at Sir James Hartingdon's house, and Mark Ferrers was with them. Jessica drove her own car, and with her she elected to have Rodrigo, while Lady Hartingdon sat between Constancia and Mark Ferrers on the back seat of Don Carlos's second, chauffeur-driven car. He himself had April in the seat beside him at the wheel of his long cream-coloured car.

But if April had imagined he might thaw on the journey—perhaps attempt an apology for his behaviour since the night of their engagement dinner—he did nothing of the kind. He had been all brilliant, caressing smiles when he saw Constancia for the first

time that day, took her in his arms and saluted the top
of her lovely dark head with a feather-like kiss, and
presented her with a morocco jeweller's case that contained a set of bracelets and a necklace made of
beaten silver and turquoise. In her delight she had
thrown her arms around his neck and kissed him
shyly but ardently—so ardently that April found it
necessary to avert her eyes—and Doña Ignatia had
decided it was a good moment to offer her own gift,
thereby making it necessary for Constancia to drop
her arms and assume a new kind of pleasure, even if
she didn't feel it.

April had done up a small gift for Constancia in an
attractive package, and when the Spanish girl opened
it she looked unexpectedly, but quite genuinely,
pleased. For the package contained some English
lawn handkerchiefs and a bottle of French perfume
which had been a gift to herself, but which she had

"Oh, but you are kind!" Constancia said quickly,
and looked, for a moment, as if she were tempted to
give April a hug too—until she remembered who she
was, and why exactly she was there. Then she
coloured and looked a little uncomfortable, and
repeated, "You are very kind. I am most grateful!"

April experienced a quick twinge of regret. If only
Constancia had been a normal ward of Don Carlos
—without any proprietorial interest in Don Carlos!—
then, she was more or less certain, the two of them
would have got on very well.

Don Carlos let his eyes rest on April for rather a
lingering moment, then he said briskly that they must
be off. Doña Ignatia came out into the courtyard to
watch their departure and wave to the two cars before

they disappeared under the arch, and then they were on their way to the Hartingdons'.

But the brief flash of good humour, the urbanity inspired by Constancia, did not survive being alone with April in a car, and even before they reached the Hartingdons' Carlos had withdrawn into his composed and self-contained shell again. He was charming to Lady Hartingdon, suave to Jessica, and then the charm evaporated, and the long drive to Granada had commenced, with polite talk concerning the countryside the only talk that took place between the Don and his bride-to-be.

They stopped for lunch in a delightful small town where the townsfolk were immensely interested in the procession of smart cars, and then continued without interruption (save one) until they reached their objective. The interruption was during the fiercest part of the afternoon, when they paused for refreshments in the cool garden of a roadside café, and Don Carlos insisted that the ladies took advantage of the interlude by reclining in rattan chairs under the protection of an age-old vine. After that he arranged with the proprietor's wife for them to wash and attend to the ravages to their complexions in one of the bedrooms of the café.

When they were on their way again April realized that, but for that interlude, she would have found the heat far more trying than she actually did—although Don Carlos's car travelled at such a speed that a constant thin current of air was churned up by their passage. And when they finally arrived in Granada she was not nearly as exhausted as she had expected to be.

There was no attempt at sight-seeing that day, for

when they arrived it was already growing dusk, and they went straight to the hotel where rooms had been reserved for them. It was a very unusual hotel, more like a centuries-old inn than a modern hotel, and it was gay within with quantities of beaten copper, brass and Moorish-style hangings, and so close to the palace of the Generalife that visitors sipping after-dinner coffee on the terrace could watch the slender green yews that rose above the palace swaying dreamily against the backcloth of starry night sky.

And in Granada the stars are so bright that the vast canopy of the sky is like a jeweller's display counter, scintillating with diamonds and plushy with velvet. The Sierra Nevada rise against the sky, an impressive sight in daylight, even more impressive when lighted by the fires of sunset, and a solid dark wall reaching for the stars when night swoops down over the fertile valley that is heavy with the scent of tobacco plantations at the closing of the day.

April was filled with admiration for the fertility of this wonderful valley, wherein the Moors set down Granada, when she saw it for the first time on the last lap of their day-long journey. She had become accustomed to the flamboyance of Andalusia, but here was a richness undreamed of, an abundance of fruit, flowers and grain. Never had she seen such golden wheat, never had she smelt such an exciting perfume as the perfume of the tobacco plantations as the light died out of the sky, and the dusk fell softly, like a gauzy mantle.

Her eyes were still wide with wonder, as well as rimmed with tiredness, when they arrived at the hotel. She was glad that everyone went straight to their rooms, and she was glad that her own had a luxurious

168

private bath, which she made immediate use of, after which she dressed for dinner in something simple and cool that had not been designed for evening, but was quite suitable after a long day devoted to travel.

When she descended to the ground floor of the hotel Lady Hartingdon and Jessica, both elaborately gowned, were sipping drinks with Don Carlos in one of the attractive public rooms that opened out on to the terrace. Beyond the windows the night was sensuously warm and still, and from the terrace came bursts of laughter, voices and the occasional popping of champagne corks and the chinking of ice against the sides of glasses.

Don Carlos stood up at once to provide April with a chair, but before she was comfortably seated Constancia joined them, wearing the bright scarlet dress which was the most colourful one in her wardrobe. She looked as gay and vivid as the dress, not a bit tired after the long journey by road, and as it was her birthday she sat opposite her guardian at the large table devoted to their party when they went in to dinner, and acted the part of hostess.

Toasts were drunk to her health and happiness, and she sparkled like the many facets of a diamond. Mark Ferrers, who sat near to her, admired her so openly with his eyes that April, seeing the way Carlos began to frown, wished she could do something to warn him to be more careful, especially as Rodrigo also began to look a trifle black. But, seated at the right hand of her fiancé, with Lady Hartingdon between her and Mark, there was nothing she could do.

The music from a nearby ballroom was most inviting, but Carlos was quite firm in his refusal to permit his ward to dance that night, after such an exhausting day, and she went quite meekly to bed at last . . . although her eyes were very bright as she sent a final, almost challenging look, at both the younger men, to be divided equally between them. And the look said plainly that she was enjoying their joint admiration.

Only April noticed that her guardian's lips grew tighter than ever. She herself made her excuses and went to bed, but she had no idea when Jessica retired . . . or whether she seized the opportunity to inveigle the host out on to the moonlit terrace to have a few words with him in private as soon as the coast was reasonably clear. For Lady Hartingdon was scarcely likely to go to the trouble of reminding her daughter that Don Carlos was engaged to be married.

But as April got into bed she thought of Jessica's gorgeous gown, her flaming red hair and her fascinating eyes, and tried not to be consumed by jealousy. She thought of Constancia, like a vivid flower in her red dress, and Carlos's smouldering look as the evening wore on... and she realized that here was something too powerful and important to evoke jealousy. It merely made her feel acutely unhappy as she lay in the darkness of her room and recalled Carlos's cool kiss on the back of her hand when he said good night.

The next day was devoted to sight-seeing, and in the brilliant sunlight—that made the light powdering of snow on the Sierra Nevada sparkle like diamond dust scattered broadcast—April had her first sight of the Alhambra, a palace of red rock well deserving to be known as "The Rosy Towers." Alhambra means red, and Don Carlos explained this to April. Then he took them into the very heart of the palace—which is, actually, three palaces, all contained within the enormously thick outer walls—and they walked in the Courtyard of Lions, and the Court of Myrtles, where strange fish disport themselves in a marble basin, tall cypresses sway dreamily against the sky, and twelve lions cast their shadows across the pavement and in so doing mark the passing of the hours.

When they emerged from the Alhambra April was confused by the colour of it, by the beauty of the gilded domes and the brilliance of the lacy stucco work inlaid with glass like precious gems, the endless corridors and the underground chambers. There was the scent of hot yew in her nostrils, the feel of hard marble beneath her feet, and she was glad of a temporary respite on the terrace of their inn, where they were restored with reviving drinks before going on to more sight-seeing. And, before lunch, she had received a vague impression of Granada, with its old Zacatin street as busy as a beehive, its silk bazaar, crowded and redolent of spicy Arab scents that emerged from strange Arab-style shops, and its many bridges that cross the famous Darro gorge. It seemed to her that Granada, in spite of its hordes of tourists, all of whom had to be housed in modern hotels, was made up of steep and narrow streets, paved with slippery round cobbles, and that for colour and picturesqueness it could outdo anything the world might have to offer.

She could see Mark Ferrers growing rapt with admiration as the hours passed, and she realized that the artist in him was in the ascendant, and that for the time being Constancia was of comparatively little interest. He talked to April because she too was full of the somewhat dazed appreciation of the foreigner, and

171

Constancia flirted outrageously with Rodrigo whenever she had the opportunity, and her guardian's back was temporarily turned to her. Jessica attached herself to the host's side, and asked him many eager questions, although she had seen the whole thing before—probably more than once!—and only Lady Hartingdon complained of the heat, and announced that she would do no more sight-seeing after lunch, and would not even put a foot outside the hotel until they left the following day.

April had the feeling—and she was probably right—that Carlos was ignoring her, in so far as his natural politeness would permit him to ignore her. He saw to it that she was never overtired, that she took advantage of every patch of shade, and sank into every vacant chair he could procure for her. But as he did precisely the same thing for all three of the other female members of his party, this did not set her apart. And, by this time, not even the knowledge that she was his fiancée had the power to fill her with anything approaching a sensation of being "set apart."

It was Constancia whom he watched, Jessica to whom he lent an attentive ear, and April for whom he had nothing but frigid politeness.

That evening they dined early, in order to be able to devote an hour or so to dancing before midnight. It was Constancia's real birthday celebration, for normally she was not permitted to dance in hotel ballrooms, and this was to mark her emancipation from sheltered girlhood. She would be permitted one or two frivolous evenings from now on, until she was handed over to the care of a husband . . . but when that event would take place no one was in a position to guess.

172

Least of all Constancia, who seemed to be really enjoying herself for the first time since April had known her.

Whether her life under the protective wing of Doña Ignatia was too narrow to allow her the opportunity to develop as normal girls develop, whether the boredom of such an existence—with few friends, constant supervision, and no outlet for natural energies—had caused her to concentrate on her guardian to such an extent that she had gradually come to convince herself that he was all-important to her, April could only begin to surmise, but since arriving in Granada she had certainly displayed an avid need for fresh experiences. She never ceased to sparkle, and if her guardian rebuked her she pouted mutinously for a moment... but it was only for a moment, and then she was gay again.

The fact that he could be displeased with her occasionally had suddenly ceased to worry her, and the fact that he was ready to spoil her if she used the right methods of coaxing obviously meant less, too. There were the two young men—Mark Ferrers and Rodrigo —both eager to compliment her and sit beside her and dance with her when permission was reluctantly granted, and even carry her out into the dusk of the hotel garden—without waiting for permission!—if she herself was willing, and the knowledge seemed to go to her head.

She was allowed one glass of champagne with her dinner, and that too seemed to go to her head. But in a way that made her violently attractive, bewitchingly beautiful, infectiously gay. She teased Don Carlos into leading her out on to the dance floor just as soon as their dinner was over, and because it was her birthday celebration the other women looked on with varying smiles of approval. April smiled because she realized Constancia was quite extraordinarily lovely, and anyone as young and lovely as she was ought to be fêted during their birthday celebration; Jessica smiled more tightly because she was supposed to be a great friend and supporter of Constancia, and there wasn't very much else she could do. Lady Hartingdon smiled because she too was enjoying herself, and Don Carlos was a wonderful host. She hadn't had such a magnificent dinner for a long time.

Rodrigo and Mark were the ones who looked on without any noticeable enthusiasm. But soon Mark was dancing with Constancia, Jessica danced with the host, and April with Rodrigo sat talking at their table on the edge of the floor. Lady Hartingdon had vanished to repair the ravages to her complexion caused by a warm night and a rather too tightly fitting dress, that brought beads of perspiration to her forehead, under her elegant hair-style.

Rodrigo looked sullen ... April had never seen him look so sullen before. He did not ask her to dance, although—doing his duty, perhaps, as a host—Carlos had passed her over in favour of Jessica when deciding to take to the glistening floor himself.

No doubt, in due course, he would return to the table and ask his fiancée to dance ... but for the moment she was a wallflower, the only one of the female members of the party who was simply hating the evening, wishing it would end. In her handbag was a letter from Señora Cortez, who sent profuse apologies from Brazil for the way she had unfortunately had to treat her excellent nannie-companion for little Juan Cortez, explaining that she was now reunited with her husband, and offering to cable funds immediately if April would consider rejoining them, and taking on her old job again.

Apparently Don Carlos had been in touch with them, but he had not informed them that he and April were now engaged to be married. And Señora Cortez, having seen to it that her husband discharged his debt to the Don by paying April's arrears of salary into his bank, could see no reason why April should not be quite glad to become a member of their family again. Only this time it would be in Brazil ... an exciting place for a young unattached girl, or so the Señora assured April.

Watching her fiancé dancing superbly with his beautiful ward—in white again tonight, with white flowers in her hair—although he was giving nothing away by his expression, April felt her fingers close over the letter inside her slim brocade handbag, and she wondered suddenly whether she ought to do something about it. Whether she ought to look upon it as a directive ... a way out of an impossible situation! A termination of that situation!

"I dislike him so thoroughly that I would like to slit his throat," Rodrigo muttered at her elbow. He was watching Mark Ferrers being charming to Jessica, but with eyes over the top of her head for Constancia. "If he were not here tonight I could enjoy myself. Constancia is changing! She is not so obsessed with my excellent half-brother, whom she has adored for so long. Tonight she is ready to be flirtatious ... and that is something! But the pity of it is there is another man for her to be flirtatious with!"

April watched Jessica and Mark Ferrers walk towards them, and she smiled deliberately up into her fellow-countryman's face. Her smile was an invitation, and he could not but ask her to dance, and she whispered in an aside to Rodrigo:

"Make the most of your opportunity! *I'll* keep Mark away from Constancia... for a while, at least!"

She managed to keep Mark away from Constancia for quite a long while, looking innocently into Don Carlos's face when he frowned blackly as he saw her accept the Englishman's invitation, and then smiling brilliantly once more up into the latter's face as they danced. She even permitted him to dance her—long before the music ceased—out on to the terrace, and in the quiet and serenity of moonlight, with dark cypresses waving above them, and on all sides of them, they disappeared into the fastness of the hotel garden.

"Whew!" Mark exclaimed, when they were well away from the hotel, and the lights of the ballroom no longer reached them. He put a finger down inside his collar as if to loosen it, and mopped at his face with a silk handkerchief. "That young woman, Constancia, has the shattering charm of quite a number of Spanish women—particularly at her age, when they're like ripe fruit dangling on a tree!—but I find that a little of them goes a long way! You..." and he looked at April's cool dark head, barely on a level with his dinner-jacketed shoulder... "thank heavens you're English, and don't expect me to make love to you. Not that I wouldn't enjoy making love to you," frankly, his eyes glistening just a little, "if we hadn't had such a day! But quite honestly, all that sight-seeing... and with your noble fiancé being so suave and smooth about everything! But when I go sight-seeing

I like to admire the things I want to admire, and preferably not in company—or not such a phalanx of company!"

"I know." April sank down on a white-painted garden seat and spread the skirts of her pink dress, that looked pale as a moth's wing in the moonlight. "That's to say, I understand what you mean, as you're an artist."

"And although you're not an artist, you're terribly soothing." He sat down beside her on the seat. "I think you feel as I do about all that colour and warmth we saw this morning, the beauty of all that Moorish craftsmanship... the urge anyone like myself has to paint, and go on painting it!"

They went on talking about Moorish craftsmanship until quite a considerable while had elapsed since they left the hotel. April appeared to be paying a great deal of attention to every sentence uttered by Ferrers, and she felt sure he was extremely flattered by her attentiveness, but what she was actually thinking about was Rodrigo... and how clever he had been at detaching Constancia from the rest of them, and carrying her off somewhere into the garden.

Her guardian might be furious—and no doubt would be when he discovered what they had been up to—but just then it didn't seem to April that Carlos had any real right to be furious, since Constancia was, after all, only his ward, and Rodrigo was in love with her. She had to marry some time, and why not Rodrigo... who was so charming and friendly, and very much in love with her?

Here April felt a sudden twinge—a little upsurging of regret because she had absolutely no right to interfere in the Don's affairs, to encourage disobedience in

177

his ward behind his back. But when it also occurred to her that Carlos, as a man betrothed had no right to feel active jealousy of any man who approached Constancia (and she was quite sure it was jealousy—naked and rather primitive) the feeling of uneasiness and betrayal slid away from her, and she became convinced that, in a way, she was doing a good thing for Constancia.

The girl was coming alive to the world about her, and she wanted to be free. And if Carlos wanted to marry her—if, that is, he would have preferred to marry her to any other woman—why then hadn't he asked her to marry him, instead of asking her, April? Why hadn't he waited for Constancia's seventeenth birthday—an age when she was ripe for wedlock, having been brought up in the south and the hot sun of Andalusia!—and asked her to marry him then?

Without complicating the lives of other people ... impressionable people like herself, who would never cease to be desperately in love with him, although she understood now that he could never be in love with her!

It was Constancia he loved! And before Constancia, it was Constancia's mother. A very natural evolution, and something that should not have been ignored, or any effort made to overcome a state of affairs that was quite inevitable!

But it made April feel lost and alone and very sick at heart as she sat there in the moonlight, listening to Mark Ferrers exclaiming over the wonders and the beauties of Granada.

She answered automatically at intervals, and she was saying to herself: "It would be the best thing in the world if I went right away ... as quickly as possible. Señora Cortez's offer is the way out!" when Carlos's voice spoke harshly behind them, and she stood up guiltily and whirled round.

"So there you both are!" Carlos's voice was full of carefully contained rage. "I've been hunting all over the grounds for you, April, and I find you here... with Señor Ferrers!"

April looked at him quietly.

"Why?" she asked. "Why have you been looking for me?"

For one instant she thought the look from his dark eyes would wither her, it was so full of concentrated resentment.

"Why?" He repeated the word icily. "Constancia and Rodrigo have both disappeared, and I am determined to find them! If you can bear to interrupt your absorbing conversation and join in the search perhaps you will be good enough to do so at once... while they are still somewhere in the immediate vicinity!"

April looked at him queerly.

"Why?" she asked again. "Are you afraid," a strange, unbalanced note of lightness entering her voice, "that they might have eloped?"

"The women of my family do not elope," he replied disdainfully.

"No," she said, while her wide eyes regarded him, and her long hair was gently stirred by the night breeze, "the women of your family do as they are told, don't they, Don Carlos? They marry when they are ordered, and they decline to marry when they are ordered!" She forgot Mark Ferrers was standing there beside her, looking increasingly uncomfortable as he became aware of his host's wrath, and because she couldn't stop the words she rushed on: "I agreed to

179

marry you because you ordered me to do so!... I don't think it ever seriously occurred to you that a refusal on my part was possible! You are the great Don Carlos de Formera y Santos who can offer so much, and I'm the little nobody who should have been overwhelmed because you offered it all to me. But I'm not! Not in the very slightest degree overwhelmed, and if I can find Constancia for you..." she turned, as if about to rush blindly off into the darkness "... then you can take it all back and offer it to her. For unless you marry Constancia, and put Rodrigo out of his misery once and for all, nobody's going to be happy... least of all me!"

She took a few steps into the darkness, but Mark Ferrers caught her wrist.

"I say, I say!" he protested. "I didn't meant to cause all this bother!..."

She wrenched away her wrist.

"You haven't caused any bother. This was something that had to happen. But I'm going to find Constancia!"

"April!" Carlos called, his voice entirely different, but she had disappeared in the blackness of the trees, and by the time he started after her she already had a good lead.

Half sobbing, more upset than she had ever been in her life, April flew down the path between the dark lines of cypresses, and when she heard him coming after her she hid behind a tree. Then she doubled back to the hotel and almost collided with Jessica Hartingdon, who was standing in the entrance. She looked as if she was trying to make up her mind about something.

CHAPTER XIV

"CONSTANCIA?" April demanded, appealingly. "Have you any idea where she is?"

Jessica smiled.

"Just gone off in a taxi to a well-known night spot... well-known in these parts, I mean. I suggested to her that she be really rash and go off and enjoy herself with Rodrigo."

April gasped.

"Carlos will never forgive her!"

Jessica smiled less pleasantly.

"That was something I had in mind," she said. "And if you," she added, "don't want to become involved in his wrath, you'd better go and bring her back, hadn't you?"

April looked bewildered.

"How...?"

Jessica indicated a taxi that had just arrived with a passenger in the forecourt.

"Take that," she suggested, "and tell the man you want to be dropped at The Golden Cockerel. It's terribly new and terribly exciting... but it won't matter that you haven't an escort if you're simply looking for Constancia. Don't spoil their sport too soon, but you'd better bring her back!"

There was a mocking note in her voice which April didn't wait to listen to further. She ran down the hotel steps and entered the taxi, giving the driver the name of The Golden Cockerel. If he looked at her a little oddly it never occurred to her, and she was too upset to realize that she was without the means of paying for the taxi when they arrived because she hadn't any money with her. All she did was grip the edge of the seat hard as the taxi shot out of the forecourt, and eventually appeared to lose itself in a maze of narrow streets which were like dark tunnels to April, although they were lighted at intervals by a lantern over a doorway, or a light that streamed from a window

The night was very hot, and through the open windows of the taxi came the all-pervading scent of tobacco-plant, as well as the heady scents of countless other flowers that bloomed in tucked away courtyards and gardens. When they flashed past the mouth of a very dark alley-way—or so it seemed to April—she caught the sound of a guitar twanging, and a man singing softly to the darkness and the night . . . almost certainly underneath a lady's window, as she realized.

Then the taxi stopped abruptly, in the very middle of that network of narrow streets. The driver got out and lifted his bonnet and looked at his engine, and when April made anxious inquiries he shrugged his shoulders. They had broken down, and he was not at all sure what the trouble was, but if she would have patience he would find out.

In desperation she stood there waiting until a long cream-coloured car came nosing its way down the narrow street, and behind the wheel she recognized Don Carlos. The most absurd panic overtook her, and without stopping to think what she was doing—and risking—she darted off down the intersecting, and even narrower way. But Carlos was out of his car and after her—to the taxi-man's utter astonishment—before she had gone twenty yards, and after forty yards he had caught her up. By that time she was in a state of panic far exceeding anything she had felt before, and this time the panic had to do with the sudden realization that had beset her that she did not know where she was going, and if she continued she would almost certainly be lost in a labyrinth of utterly strange houses, and even more alien people. Lost, and without any money, and in a filmy evening dress!

She turned just as Carlos caught up with her, and in a state of wild, unreasoning fear she threw herself into his arms. She burst into a torrent of weak sobs, and he held her protectively close. It didn't matter to her now that he might be angry with her, but it astounded her that he could be so wonderfully, exquisitely tender and understanding.

"I was so afraid!" she sobbed. "I suddenly realized that I'd lost my way..."

He stroked her hair with a hand that trembled slightly.

"*Amada*," he demanded softly, "do you think I would allow you to be lost? I came after you at once, and I saw you as soon as you slipped out of the taxi. But oh, my heart," reproachfully, "why did you run from me? Why did you run away from me at all?"

"It was Constancia," she replied, leaning against him in luxurious abandon, while they were both surrounded by the darkness of the night—and, not far away, the man with the delightful tenor voice went on singing, to the accompaniment of his guitar. "She—she has gone to a place called The Golden Cockerel ... with Rodrigo. I—I was going after them, to bring her back."

"Oh, *amada*," he said again—and there was no mistake now, his voice trembled. "But Constancia is at the hotel, and Mark Ferrers—who, Jessica suggested, should come after you—is there too. It was a whimsical idea on the part of Miss Hartingdon... that I should get the impression you and Ferrers had arranged to meet away from the hotel. But, unfortunately for her, I happen to know you better than she does, and it was I who came after you!"

She put back her head and looked up at him, her eyes bright with tears. The pale rays of a street lamp showed him quite clearly her tear-streaked face.

"But—but why?" she stammered. "Why did she...?"

He shrugged.

"Women are inexplicable sometimes." That was all he permitted himself to say about Jessica Hartingdon. "And now I will take you back, my dear one."

April borrowed his handkerchief and wiped away a tear. He would have done it for her gladly, but she preferred to keep her face hidden just then.

"You said... you said Constancia is at the hotel?"

"Yes."

"And... Rodrigo?"

"Is with her. They never left the gardens. Of course, she would never have dreamed of leaving them without my permission. And, contrary to some strange idea you seem to have formed, I do not wish to offer her all I possess... I have already offered it to you. And you are the woman I love... no," correcting himself with great soberness, "adore! I wonder if you have the faintest idea how I felt just now when I saw you rush blindly away from me into the darkness of

184

these narrow streets rather than be seen by me? I wonder if you know how much you hurt me tonight when you spoke as you did in front of your countryman, Ferrers!"

She looked up at him this time in a kind of glorious bewilderment. She was trembling with unbelief and the desire to press closer to him, to be taken even more possessively into his arms.

"Oh, Carlos, I never thought ... I mean I thought it was Constancia you ... well, you would rather have married, although perhaps you had some reason for not doing so. I thought you only asked me to marry you because ... well, it was a way out of a difficulty ... a sensible solution to a problem!"

"Instead of which," taking her face between his hands and devouring it with his eyes, "I asked you to marry me because ..." And then he caught himself up sharply. "But you shall say it first! You have treated me abominably—not only tonight, but for several days past!—and now you shall tell me why *you* agreed to marry me. It was not because I forced you to, *amada*"—his lips twisting wryly at the remembrance of things she had said to him—"for you are not a young woman to be forced! If you were, I would not have felt this wild desire to make you my wife! Now tell me, why did you agree to marry me?"

She felt, as she had felt once before, as if her whole being was eager to be dissolved in his.

"Oh, Carlos," she breathed, her eyes hanging upon his in the lamplight, "it was because I love you. I love you so very much, Carlos, and I—I think I must have done so ... always!"

She heard him utter a sound like a long-drawn-out "A-ah!", and then he was holding her fiercely in his arms, caring little if anyone saw them, aware only of the flaming love-light in her eyes, the eager lips upraised to his. And when he finally lifted his head and drew a deep breath after devouring her mouth with his own the stars were spinning round April, and the dark street was a corner of paradise.

"We will go now, my darling," he said. He looked round him regretfully. "Although I shall probably never know a happier moment than this place has afforded me."

He led her back to the car, and when he had put her into the seat beside the driving-seat he got in beside her and took her quite naturally into his arms. The taxi-man had somehow or other repaired his taxi and driven off into the night, and they were still alone in a corner of Granada that seemed to them both like a lost world at that late hour of the night . . . or rather, morning. For, when she glanced at the clock on the dashboard, April saw that it was nearly three a.m.

"Darling," Don Carlos said, as if he liked the sound of the English endearment, lifting her chin with his long brown fingers and looking at her adoringly, "we will have no more of Constancia, is that agreed? No more unhappiness about her, I mean? Tonight I told Rodrigo that he can marry her in a year's time, but not before . . . I simply will not permit her to marry before she is eighteen. She is still a child to me, you know."

"And I thought——"

"I know what you thought! But that was because I did not tell you the truth, that I recovered from my infatuation for Constancia's mother long, long ago. She was but an infatuation, you know . . . I was a boy in love with a woman far older than himself. And when I grew up I knew that when, and if, I fell in love again, it would be a very different thing . . . not woman-worship, but a man's desire for a woman! The years passed, and it did not seem to me that I would find my love . . . until that afternoon in Madrid, when I saw her standing anxiously in the hall of an empty flat, her hair like sunshine all about her! And then I think my heart dropped right out at your feet, and I wanted you more than anything else in life."

She gazed up at him in astonishment.

"But I thought you regarded me as a perfect nuisance! . . . I thought you asked me to marry you simply and solely to . . . because you thought you had compromised me!"

"Or you had compromised me?" He smiled, but his smile was very tender. "Even in Spain we do not go.to such extreme lengths, my dear one, unless we are sure that the woman is an excellent match, and will make an ideal wife for the most prosaic of reasons, or because she is as necessary as breathing. Because we are in love!"

"And in your case, since no one could possibly regard me as an excellent match . . . ?" She waited breathlessly.

"In my case, it was because I couldn't live without you! Because you were, possibly, even more necessary than breathing! Oh, *amada*," his voice meltingly soft, "when a man and a woman meet and fall in love, as we did—though without admitting it one to the other!—there is only one thing to be done, and that is to put each other out of their agony by getting married. And you and I will be married at the very earliest moment that I can arrange it. I will not run the risk of having you run away from me again!"

She nestled her head into his shoulder.

"I could never, never run away from you now!"

"Do not worry," said Carlos, in his old, autocratic voice. "You will not be allowed to!"

FREE! Harlequin Romance Catalogue

Here is a wonderful opportunity to read many of the Harlequin Romances you may have missed.

The HARLEQUIN ROMANCE CATALOGUE lists hundreds of titles which possibly are no longer available at your local bookseller. To receive your copy, just fill out the coupon below, mail it to us, and we'll rush your catalogue to you!

Following this page you'll find a sampling of a few of the Harlequin Romances listed in the catalogue. Should you wish to order any of these immediately, kindly check the titles desired and mail with coupon.

GOLDEN HARLEQUIN LIBRARY

Now 18 Volumes!

FIFTY-FOUR

Harlequin readers will be delighted! We've collected ~~thirty-six~~ of your all-time favourite Harlequin Romance novels to present to you in an attractive new way. It's the Golden Harlequin Library.

Each volume contains three complete, unabridged Harlequin Romance novels, most of which have not been available since the original printing Each volume is exquisitely bound in a fine quality rich gold hardcover with royal blue imprint. And each volume is priced at an unbelievable $1.75. That's right! Handsome, hardcover library editions at the price of paperbacks!

This very special collection of ~~12~~ 18 volumes (there'll be more!) of classic Harlequin Romances would be a distinctive addition to your library. And imagine what a delightful gift they'd make for any Harlequin reader!

Start your collection now. See reverse of this page for full details.